THE SILVER COBWEB

A small-town girl had been murdered by a hired killer from New York. It made no sense to me . . . but there it was. A murder. We had apprehended the killer and that part was over. It was not a question of who had committed the crime. The big question would be why. It would take time and a lot of trouble to find that out.

Famous books and authors in the Fontana Series

The
Silver Cobweb

BEN BENSON

COLLINS

fontana books

First published 1956
First issued in Fontana Books 1958

PRINTED IN GREAT BRITAIN
COLLINS CLEAR-TYPE PRESS : LONDON AND GLASGOW

CHAPTER ONE

IT WAS A TROOPER named Keith Ludwell who was first on the murder scene. He had been on patrol a mile south of the town when he received the radio call rushing him in his cruiser to the Fedder house at 12 Montague Street, Dorset. He arrived there two minutes after the murderer drove away in his blue truck.

Just minutes previously, the neighbours on Montague Street had seen pretty, twenty-one-year-old Mary Ann Fedder driving her little Nash at great speed to her house. Behind her was the blue panel truck. Mary Fedder had left her car, raced into her house and slammed the door shut.

Moments later the sergeant at the State Police barracks in Topsfield had received Mary Ann's urgent, hysterical call that somebody was trying to kill her. While she was on the telephone talking to the sergeant, the murderer had broken the door down and had fired four shots at her. The man ran out and drove away. The gathering neighbours had seen the murderer, the truck and the licence plate. But because the man was armed with a pistol nobody had dared make a move to stop him.

When Trooper Ludwell arrived the frantic people were out on the sidewalk in front of the house, pointing in the direction where the truck had disappeared, shouting the licence number and yelling about the shots that had been fired.

I know Keith Ludwell would have liked nothing better than to chase the murderer. He couldn't, of course. His first job was to render all possible aid to the victim. So Ludwell, being a meticulous trooper, ignored the neighbours and ran into the house to Mary Ann Fedder. He saw her bullet-torn face, the wide-open staring eyes and knew she was dead and there was no help to be given. He had immediately phoned Sergeant Bart Neal at the barracks. Neal told him to stay there with the body.

It was 2.04 on Tuesday afternoon in the fourth week of May and, at the time, I was on a routine patrol six miles west of Dorset near Dorset Pond. At 2.01, on my short-wave radio, I had heard the Signal 16 to Ludwell. But because the message wasn't for me I hadn't paid much attention to it.

Now at 2.04 my radio box said tersely, " K2. Special attention Cruiser 27. Be on the lookout for a blue GMC panel truck, Mass. registration Bo662. Occupant reported to have shot and killed Mary Ann Fedder in Dorset five minutes ago. Last seen heading west on Route 110 in the direction of Georgetown. Please acknowledge."

That was mine. I picked up the handphone, pressed the button and said, " Received okay. Twenty-seven, off."

I was on Pond Road at the time near the junction of Route 110. The car I was driving, Cruiser 27, was a souped-up interceptor and was capable of overtaking any commercial car or truck on the road. As I moved quickly out into the intersection to set up a roadblock a blue panel truck flashed by me. The hatless man bent over the wheel ignored my blasting horn. I

caught a glimpse of the number plate as it rushed by—
Bo662.

I picked up the handphone and said, " Cruiser 27
to K2. I just spotted that blue truck at the Dorset
line and I'm chasing it west on 110." Then I turned
the cruiser after it, my roof blinker on, siren wailing.
Over the radio speaker I heard the dispatcher calling
our Andover Barracks to send cruisers to converge, and
also messages to the local police in Georgetown,
Haverhill and Lawrence.

Route 110 had some bad curves, and the truck
yawed and careened wildly from one side of the
highway to the other. It wasn't until we hit a stretch
of straight road that I was able to pull alongside the
truck and motion it over. By that time I had taken
my service revolver out of the flap holster and had
laid it on the seat beside me. The driver ignored my
order to stop and tried to get more speed out of the
truck. So, riding parallel to him, I reached down,
picked up the revolver and aimed it at his head. He
took a quick look at it and jammed on his brakes. The
truck slowed to a stop. As it did, his door flew open
and he ran out. He ducked around the truck and
fled into the woods.

I parked behind the truck, then ran across the
shoulder of the road after him. The man was about
twenty yards ahead. I shouted to him to stop. He
paid no attention. I fired one shot into the air. He kept
running, trying to zigzag a little. I closed in on him,
raising my revolver again and cocking it.

There was a steep little gully ahead and a little brook
running at the bottom of it. The man paused at the
top of the gully, turned and pulled an automatic

pistol from his pocket. As he brought it up, aiming it at me with both hands, he stumbled. Falling backwards, he rolled down the gully to the edge of the stream.

I came down the gully and dived for him. He lost his grip on the pistol. As he scrabbled for it, I swung the revolver, hitting him with the barrel across the side of the head. Because I had my finger on the trigger, the jarring blow set the gun off. I had a bad, frightened moment then, thinking I had shot the man. But the bullet only grazed his hair.

" Don't shoot me," he panted. " Don't shoot. I quit."

By that time I had twisted him face down in the soft marshy earth and dead leaves. With one knee in his back I took my handcuffs out of the black leather case and locked his arms behind him. My hands patted his clothes for another weapon. Then I picked up the automatic pistol and tucked it into my gun-belt.

" All right," I said, yanking him to his feet. " Up."

He said, " Don't shoot, trooper. I'm giving you no trouble."

I was breathing heavily and said nothing. He didn't look like a murderer. He was a pudgy little man about thirty-five, his hair a silky brown. Part of his moonlike, round face had dirt and dead leaves clinging to it. His lips were small and full and his eyes were mild and an almost colourless brown. The blow from my gun had raised a large red welt along his left temple.

I prodded him up the gully and to the cruiser. I pushed him into the back seat, then picked up the phone and reported to the barracks. Sergeant Neal told me to stand by. He would send two men to assist me.

When I put the phone down the man said in a soft voice, " What's your name, trooper? "

" Lindsey," I said. " Ralph Lindsey. What's yours, mister? "

" Arnold Johnson," he said. " I guess there's some mistake, sonny. You scared me, chasing after me and pointing that big revolver like I did something wrong. How about getting these handcuffs off? They're hurting me."

" Save it, Johnson."

" No, I mean it," he said. " There's a mistake somewhere. Maybe I know what it is. You're looking for a blue panel truck. Probably stolen. It passed me on the road going like a bat out of hell. A truck just like mine. You missed it, sonny."

" I didn't miss that gun you were aiming at me, Johnson."

" Aiming? " He laughed apologetically. " You have it wrong, Lindsey. I wasn't going to argue with you. I was holding the gun out to give to you." He edged over on the seat, turned and pushed his wrists out. " Take them off, kid. You made a mistake and I'm willing to forget it. You've still got a chance of catching the other truck."

" You stay there," I said, " or I'll clout you again."

" So your name's Lindsey," he said gently. " I'm going to remember it real good, sonny."

Troopers Tony Pellegrini and Ed Doherty came a few minutes later. Doherty would stay with the truck until the technical men arrived to examine it. Pellegrini and I drove the murderer to the barracks.

We kept the prisoner in the guardroom while Sergeant Neal was busy in the duty office with the radio, telephone and teletype. He had to call the labs. men, ballistics and photography at G.H.Q. in Boston. There were also calls to the troop commander in Framingham and the technical sergeant there. Then he had to contact the medical examiner, the district attorney and the State Police detective-lieutenants in Salem and Lawrence. Within an hour the barracks would be jammed with all sorts of police officials and witnesses. This was the quiet time and it wouldn't last long.

The murderer, handcuffed, sat at the long table, his face calm and placid and a little pale except for the mark where I had struck him. Neal, towering and burly, looked down at him.

" What's his name? " Neal asked me.

" Arnold Johnson," I said.

" Johnson," Neal said. " He looks familiar and his name isn't Johnson." He turned to the man and prodded him with a big finger. " What's your real name? "

" Arnold Johnson," the man said expressionlessly. " There's a big mistake, Sergeant."

" Let me have his wallet," Neal said.

I fished in Johnson's pocket and brought out a black pin-seal wallet. Neal examined it.

" Six hundred and twelve bucks," Neal said. " A big roll. A Mass. driver's licence made out to Arnold Johnson of Jemingway Street, Boston. The name and description look altered. A receipt from an autos.

rental agency in Boston for the truck. Registration Bo662. There's no mistake there, Johnson."

"Yes, there is," Johnson said.

"Ralph," Neal said to me, "he goes into a cell where we'll search him."

I took Johnson to the cellblock. Pellegrini opened the grilled door. In the cellblock corridor, Neal motioned for my revolver. I handed it to him and he passed it to Pellegrini.

Neal said, "Ralph, put him in the first cell and unlock the cuffs. You, Tony, stay outside the cellblock door. If this bum so much as blinks an eyelash, shoot him."

I took Johnson into the first cell and unlocked the handcuffs. From the corridor, Neal said, "Johnson, take off every stitch of clothes. I want to see you looking like a plucked chicken."

The man sat down on the hard wooden bench in the cell and rubbed his wrists for a moment. Then he began to unbutton his jacket.

I stood over him and took each article of clothing as he removed it, passing it to Neal outside. Neal examined everything closely, probing sleeve linings, seams, cuffs and shoulder pads. On the cement floor of the corridor was a little pile of coins, a set of keys and a long, wicked-looking switchknife. Neal took the belt from the trousers and the lacings from the shoes. Then he threw the trousers and shoes back into the cell. He also threw in an undershirt.

"Stay here," Neal said to me. He motioned to Pellegrini to unlock the cellblock door, then went out. I watched Johnson shake his head pityingly as he slipped on the pants and undershirt.

Neal came back. He was not wearing his pocket revolver now. In his hand was an F.B.I. flyer with two holes punched along the top. He looked at the picture on it, front and side view. " Your name isn't Johnson," he said. " It's Kurt 'Whitey' Swenke. Torpedo. New York and New Jersey. Wanted by the New York Police on three warrants of murder. A hired killer. What have you got to say now, Swenke? "

Swenke looked down at his hands, smiled slightly and said nothing.

Neal's face turned red. He reached into the cell and grabbed Swenke by the undershirt. " All right, you came to a small town and killed a harmless young girl. Now suppose you tell us why, Whitey."

" I didn't do it," Swenke said.

" Maybe you didn't understand me," Neal said. " This was no girl from the turf. This was an innocent kid. Where did you come into her life, Whitey? "

Swenke turned his face up and his mild eyes were slightly watery. " You're making a big mistake, Sergeant. I don't know anything about it. And I might get a notion to sue you guys. You can't do this to me on a little speeding charge. This truck passed me, a blue panel truck just like mine. He was going very fast——"

Neal motioned with his head to me. I left the cell. Neal stepped back quickly and clanged the cell door shut. Swenke's hands clasped the bars and he said, " I'm no trouble, Sergeant. I wouldn't even bother you for a cigarette. I don't drink and I don't smoke. I live clean and I mind my own business. And I don't know what you guys are trying to pull on me. I haven't shot anybody."

Neal turned his back. We went out of the cellblock together. Neal said, " Ralph, tell the cook to get some pots of coffee going. Pretty soon we'll be jammed to the rafters with brass."

" Right," I said. I retrieved my revolver from Pellegrini and headed through the dining-room to the kitchen. I was thinking of Mary Ann Fedder, who was dead now. I don't know why—I had never met or seen her—but I pictured her as blonde, blue-eyed and petite. A small-town girl who had been murdered by a hired killer from New York. It made no sense to me. It made no sense to Bart Neal. But there it was. A murder. We had apprehended the killer and that part was over. It was not a question of who had committed the crime. The big question would be why.

It would take time and a lot of trouble to find that out.

CHAPTER TWO

THAT NIGHT I went on patrol with Keith Ludwell, who was my room-mate. I was still in my probationary period and Ludwell, being senior man, was driving the cruiser.

" What colour hair did Mary Fedder have? " I asked him.

" Blonde. Why? "

" I just had an idea it was blonde," I said. " Blue-eyed? "

" Yes."

" Small girl? "

"Not too big."

"Funny," I said. "That's how I pictured her."

"She was going to be married in a couple of weeks," Ludwell said. "A June bride."

"That's rough," I said. "Who was the groom?"

"A local kid named Russell Westlake."

"That's rough," I said again.

"It is," Ludwell said. Then he told me how he had stood guard over Mary Ann Fedder's body, keeping the neighbours out of the house. A few minutes later Mr. and Mrs. Fedder, the parents of Mary Ann, had come bursting in. He had moved them gently but firmly into another room so they wouldn't disturb anything. It seems there had been a wedding rehearsal at the church and they had been waiting for Mary Ann to come there when they heard the news of her murder. Mrs. Fedder had become so hysterical with grief that Ludwell had had to restrain her physically until a doctor came. The doctor had given her a sedative.

"What could I do?" Ludwell said. "Sure, I felt sorry for Mrs. Fedder. But I had to preserve everything until the medical examiner and the detectives came. She kept fighting me, clawing at me, trying to get into the living-room where her dead daughter was. I couldn't let her, of course."

I nodded. That would be Keith Ludwell, I thought. Painstaking, methodical, very serious. Do everything according to the book and you'll never go wrong. He was a stickler for the rules and regulations. I was only a few months out of the State Police Academy and only five days at the Topsfield Barracks. That was why they thought it best to assign me to a man like Ludwell for instruction during my probationary period.

Ludwell drove slowly along Route 1 and the subject changed to Whitey Swenke. Neither of us had a logical answer as to his motive for killing the girl, or why he was in Dorset driving a rented truck.

It was about 9.00 p.m. and we were still talking about Swenke when a red convertible passed us going about seventy miles an hour.

We gave chase to it. By the time we caught up with the car it has passed the Topsfield Barracks and had gone a mile beyond. As we came alongside I motioned to the single occupant to pull over and stop. The driver of the car was a girl, and she stared at me with her crimson mouth startled and open. She looked at the two-tone blue cruiser and made a grimace. Slowing her car drastically, she turned it on to the shoulder of the road, the tyres screeching and gouging into the gravel.

" You take it," Ludwell said to me.

I knew in advance that it would be done strictly by the book and Ludwell would be watching me carefully. He parked directly behind the girl with our roof blinker on as a safety precaution against collisions. Our headlights would be focused on the car so that the occupant would be caught in the glare and would have to turn around to face us. That would rule out any element of surprise on her part.

I got out. As I came by the rear licence plate of the convertible I checked it in my mind with the stolen car list on our patrol card. The red convertible wasn't listed.

I went along the driver's side of the car, taking a look inside, making sure nobody was crouched in the back hiding. Then I moved to the driver's window and asked the girl for her licence and registration.

She reached for the glove compartment, took out an envelope and handed it to me. Her papers were in order. Her name was Amy Bell. She was twenty-seven years old and her address was 52 Elm Street, Dorset, Mass.

As I studied her papers in the beam of the cruiser's headlights she laughed suddenly. I looked at her and she said, " Aren't you taking a chance being out here all alone, honey child? What if I was a notorious criminal? I might have reached into that glove compartment and brought out a gun."

" You'd have had your head blown off, ma'am," I said. " There's another trooper standing at the back of your car and he's there to watch what you do."

She turned her head quickly and saw Ludwell standing at the rear right fender of her car, where he had a good view of the inside.

She smiled and nodded. " Clever, clever."

I took out my violation book. " You were going seventy miles an hour, ma'am. This is a forty-five-mile zone. Your speed was much too fast." I began to write on the slip.

She became angry. " I was late for work," she said. " Dammit, there are hardly any cars on the road."

" There are a lot of intersections," I said. " A car could come out of any one of them and not realise you were going so fast. At that speed somebody might have been killed and it could have been you. You watch the signs from now on, ma'am. The speed limits are posted."

She became angrier. I wrote " summons " at the

bottom left-hand corner of the serially-numbered slip, signed my name and gave her the white copy and her envelope. By this time Ludwell had checked the front of her car for her safety inspection sticker and had gone back to the cruiser to listen for radio calls.

I remember her holding the slip in her hand telling me just what she thought of me. I stood there and grinned a little at her fiery temper. Even in the darkness I could see she was very pretty. Black, glossy hair, a little wind-blown and cropped unevenly in front because that seemed to be the prevailing style. She had large dark eyes, a clear-white unblemished skin and a winsome, elfish face. Then I reminded myself I should go back to the cruiser. I turned away.

She had been looking at the slip and she suddenly called, " *Ralph* Lindsey? "

I went back to her open window. She said, " You *are* Lindsey, aren't you? "

" Yes, ma'am," I said.

" You don't know me," she said, giving me a lovely smile. " But I know a friend of yours, Carl Podre. You know Carl, don't you? "

" Yes," I said briefly.

" Carl told me about you," she said chattily. " He understood you were being assigned to the Topsfield Barracks. I wasn't sure it was you until I saw your name on this ticket. But now that I remember, Carl said you were young, tall and had light hair. All the description fits, doesn't it? "

" Well, yes," I said. " Pretty close."

" I sing at Carl's place. The Red Wheel. It's down the road in Dorset." She shrugged her shoulders delicately. " Dorset is where that terrible murder happened to-day. But, of course, you must know all about it."

"Yes," I said.

"I was in Boston all day and I saw it in to-night's papers." She laughed. "Now that was silly of me, wasn't it? Imagine asking *you* if you knew about it. Why, you're the very one who captured the killer, aren't you?"

"Yes."

"Bravo," she said. Then she pushed out the white slip towards me. "I hate to be a nuisance. Really, I do. But be an angel and take care of this for me, will you?"

"I'm afraid I can't. You're already booked, Miss Bell. After all, you were going over seventy."

"But I'm a friend of Carl's——"

"Sorry," I said, edging away. "These violations can't be fixed."

She crumpled the slip in her hand. "Oh, dammit," she exploded. "What a chicken outfit. You ask a man for a teeny-weeny favour and he gives you the fish eye. Where do they get you troopers? Out of a cold-storage vault?"

I grinned. "I can feel a big chill right now."

"Lindsey," she said, "you can go straight to hell." With that she jammed her foot on the starter. The car wheels spit gravel and dust as she gunned the motor and swept off down the road.

I walked back to the cruiser and got in beside Ludwell. He shook his head and frowned. "You ought to cut that stuff out," he said in his dead, quiet voice. "We're supposed to book the violation and get away. No small-talk with motorists."

"I know," I said. "But she began to talk about a mutual friend. I couldn't cut her off."

"Everybody has a mutual friend."

"This is a fellow named Carl Podre. You know him, Keith?"

"I've heard of him and I've seen him around. He owns a dine-and-dance spot called The Red Wheel." Ludwell pushed back his visored cap. "How did you book the girl?"

"Summons."

"Oh," he said.

"You surprised?"

"I was just wondering. If this Podre was such a personal friend of yours you didn't have to make it a court case. You could have given her a break and written out a warning."

"What would you have done, Keith, if you were me?"

"Just what you did. A summons. She was doing seventy. Every time I feel like easing up I see an accident with a couple of dead bodies in it. Nine times out of ten it's caused by high speed. It brings me back to my senses. But, of course, I don't know how much this friendship of Carl Podre means to you."

"Podre's no particular friend of mine." I didn't say anything more about it. There was no need explaining to Keith Ludwell that Carl Podre came from my neighbourhood in Cambridge and that I had no particular liking for him. Podre was a good eight years older than I. His kid brother, Paul, and I had been pretty friendly. Paul Podre and I both went to war in Korea, but with different outfits. Paul never came back. He was killed near Old Baldy.

I hadn't seen Carl Podre for years. I remember, in my younger days, when I was ten or so, Carl was a sharply dressed, smooth-faced kid of eighteen. You could always see him hanging around the poolroom, where he was able to pick up a little money at Kelly pool or snooker. His brother Paul could always touch him for a couple of nickels when the ice-cream man came around. I don't remember that Carl Podre had any trade or profession. It was always some kind of fringe job. Once, I recall, he was a candy hawker at the Old Howard Theatre when that burlesque house was running in Scollay Square, Boston. Later, I heard he had a small photo concession at a second-rate night club. Then I heard he had gone into horse racing. Whether he was a bookie or a tout or a horse handler I didn't know. There were rumours that he had been ruled off the tracks for some violation or other. The idea was that Carl Podre was always on the edge of things, balancing on a tightrope. Nothing he had done could be classified as exactly illegal, but nothing he did was really straightforward or substantial, either. He would disappear from Cambridge for long stretches of time, then occasionally drift back to see his folks. I don't know why he bothered. He never stayed home long. From the way his folks lived he certainly did nothing to contribute to their support.

But Carl Podre didn't stay in my mind very long. Another person kept creeping in. The beautiful, volatile Amy Bell.

CHAPTER THREE

IT WAS THREE HOURS later, around midnight, when Ludwell and I drove into the town of Dorset. First Ludwell drove me down tree-lined Montague Street.

"That's the house," Ludwell said, driving by slowly. "Nice little house. Nice little town. Nice people. It's a crying shame."

I was surprised to hear him say it. Until then I had thought Ludwell had no emotions whatsoever.

I looked at the Fedder house. It was a small, white Cape Cod cottage. On the front lawn was a pair of big elm trees. The windows of the house were lighted. There were some people on the sidewalk. Cars were parked on both sides of the street. I recognised two unobtrusive black State Police cruisers, the kind without markings, which were used for investigation work. It meant detectives and technical men were still around the Fedder house. In comparison to those two black cruisers our own patrol cruiser stood out like a Christmas tree. The patrol cruisers were painted light and dark blue, had a chrome-plated roof blinker which threw a blue light in front and a red light in back. The door panels carried the state seals, and the rear deck had large white letters that said *Massachusetts State Police*. You could spot them a mile away. Motorists seeing the plainly marked patrol cruisers would slow down and that, in turn, helped cut down on accidents.

Ludwell circled the block and drove to Dorset

Square. It was there that I saw The Red Wheel for the first time. It was set behind trim, high boxed hedges, a long, low building with a pitched roof. The shingles were painted a smoke grey and in each of the small windows was a pale-glowing, simulated candle light. Out front was a huge red neon sign in the shape of a wheel. Beside the building was a large parking lot. In the parking area were a number of cars, many of them with out-of-state tags.

"Podre does a nice business for a small town," I said to Ludwell.

"He gets the horsy crowd," Ludwell explained. "A lot of race-track people. Then, of course, a murder always brings out a morbid crowd. Holiday stuff like an old-fashioned Wild West hanging."

"It takes all kinds to make a world," I said.

"Too many of the wrong kind," Ludwell said unctuously.

Across the street from The Red Wheel parking area was a shiny green-and-white-front diner. Ludwell pulled the cruiser up along it and turned off the motor. "This is where I usually eat, Ralph," he said. "You want to go in first?"

"No, go ahead," I said. "I'm not very hungry."

Ludwell got out of the cruiser. I looked at him in the light. He was not as tall as I. Five ten and a half, possibly five-eleven. I had seen him in the shower room and I knew that under that tailored uniform was a hard-muscled, wiry body. He had a lean, almost rawboned face and a hard little chin. A face that had a hungry, impatient look all the time.

He took a white flannel cloth from the big patch pocket of his pale blue tunic and wiped the dust from

the black leather visor of his cap. Then he bent down
and dusted his black boots. He brushed his dark blue
breeches, straightened his gunbelt and crossbelt, gave
his tunic a tug and squared his cap before going into
the diner. I began to suspect there was a girl in his
life.

There was. Through the big window I could see a
green-smocked young waitress come bustling over to
him. Ludwell moved into a booth and I saw the girl
lean forward, all excited, words streaming endlessly
from her mouth. No doubt she was talking about the
murder of Mary Ann Fedder. But it wasn't just her
talking that drew my attention. She had the avid,
yearning look of a woman very much in love.

I sat there in the cruiser, sneaking a smoke, my
cigarette butt down out of sight where nobody could
see it. The short-wave radio sputtered every few
minutes but none of the calls were for us. I watched
the diner, seeing the waitress now sitting in the booth
with Ludwell. She was talking earnestly and express-
ively, and Ludwell was nodding his head once in a while
and eating slowly with that solemn, serious expression
on his face. I figured he would be in there exactly
fifteen minutes, no more and no less. The midnight
snack usually took a half-hour and was split between
the two men on patrol. It was the only meal we ate
away from the barracks.

I hadn't been paying much attention to The Red
Wheel across the street. Cars had been pulling in and
out and people had been coming and going, and I had
noticed them only casually. But I perked up when I
heard loud voices and saw a boy coming out of the
entrance. The boy was very drunk and with him was a

young, taffy-haired bobby-soxer. Neither of them looked over seventeen. The girl was trying to escort the boy to the car. Apparently he didn't want to go. The girl was loudly persistent about it.

I looked at the diner again. Ludwell was still in there drinking his coffee and the waitress was sitting closer to him, talking in the same earnest way. After a moment I picked up the handphone and told the dispatcher that Cruiser 29 was going off the air. I waited for the acknowledgment, then got out of the cruiser and crossed the road.

At the edge of the parking area was a big black Cadillac sedan with a doctor's emblem attached to the licence plate. The taffy-haired girl was trying to push the boy into the front seat. He was giggling about it. When the girl heard my footsteps she turned swiftly. Her mouth popped open and she said, " Oh, my lord. The State Police."

" What's the trouble? " I asked her.

" Nothing," she said. " I'm trying to take Dickie home."

" And who's Dickie? "

" This clown," she said, her mouth making a little moue of disgust. " Richard Cleves, Junior."

" He looks very drunk."

" Are you kidding? He's squiffed, pie-eyed, blotto."

" I'd like to see his identification."

" It's in his wallet, sir."

" Take it out, please."

She bent over and reached into the boy's pants' pocket. He brought his hands up in feeble protest but she slapped them away sharply. I don't know why it is but the maturity of a seventeen-year-old girl is much more than a boy's at the same age. She knew just what to do and was quite competent about it.

I looked at the driver's licence under the neon light. It was made out to Richard Cleves, Jr., 2 Terrace Lane, Danvers, Mass. His age was seventeen.

" Where's the car registration? " I asked.

She handed that to me. It was in the name of Dr. Richard Cleves of the same address. I wrote it in my book and handed it back. Then I reached in, pulled young Cleves out of the car and yanked him to his feet. He stared with glazed eyes at my uniform and began to babble apologies.

The girl said worriedly, " What are you doing, sir? "

" You just came out of The Red Wheel, didn't you? "

" Yes," she said. " But——"

I didn't listen to any explanation. I walked Cleves to the entrance of The Red Wheel. The young girl dog-trotted after me. Cleves was mumbling some kind of protest but I didn't pay attention. I opened the door, took Cleves by the shoulder and waltzed him inside.

There was a thickly padded rug under my feet. I was in the foyer. To the left was the taproom and to the right was the checkroom. Directly ahead was the main dining-room, with rows of booths along both sides and small white-clothed tables in the centre. I saw a head waiter's high desk and a startled, bald-headed man there in a white dinner jacket. He began to hurry towards me.

At the far end of the room was a stage. On it, alone in the glare of a baby spotlight, a girl sat at a piano. She was playing softly, singing into a microphone in a husky, vibrant voice. She was good at it. Not only in my own opinion. The diners and the waiters thought so, too. I could tell that from the rapt attention and from the absence of noise or clacking dishes.

The girl was Amy Bell. She was wearing a black lace gown. Her shoulders were bare, her black glossy hair contrasting vividly with her white skin.

The bald headwaiter was asking me anxiously what was wrong. At the same time one of the diners closest to us turned and noticed the huddle. There were whispers, a turning of bodies and heads, a scraping of chairs. A hum of voices ran through the dining-room. Amy Bell stopped playing. She brought a hand up and shaded her eyes from the bright light. I saw her looking at me. A mischievous smile wreathed her face. She banged heavily on the piano and played a loud funeral march.

The crowd tittered at first, then burst into laughter and clapped their hands. Colour rushed over my neck and face. I stood there gripping Cleves with a moist hand, feeling silly. Then I began to get angry because these callous people were laughing and joking when only a few hours ago and a few blocks away a young bride-to-be had been murdered. Because in a little cottage, almost within sound of their gleeful cackling, a mother was under a sedative because of shock. I was also angry at Amy Bell for mocking me. And I wanted to lash out at somebody for serving liquor to a seventeen-year-old boy.

A long, lanky bartender with sandy hair came out of the taproom and joined the headwaiter. The bartender said, " What's the trouble, Officer? "

" Do you remember this boy? " I asked harshly.

" Sure. He was just in here and——"

" I found him outside," I snapped. " He's stinking

drunk. Not only are you in a jam for serving a minor, but it might cost this place its licence."

"Now wait a minute," the bartender said affably. "We didn't serve the kid. He came in here drunk and we shooed him out."

A hand tapped my shoulder and a voice said, "Ralphie."

I turned and saw Carl Podre. The years had changed him. His face was not as bland and smooth, but paler, more sharpened and more dissipated. His hair had thinned and receded from his forehead, making him look a good five years older than his thirty-one years. His eyes were harder, colder, with small pouches under them. He was wearing a white dinner jacket and a narrow black bow tie.

"Ralphie boy," he said, groping for my free hand and shaking it. "Long time no see. How's your mom and dad?"

"Hold it a minute, Carl." I turned to the girl. "Was your boy friend drunk when he came in here?"

"I was trying to tell you he was," she said. "Nobody served Dickie. He came in to get liquor and they made us leave."

I felt my face flush again. I wanted to get out of there quickly. "Okay," I said to the girl. "Let's go."

But Carl Podre was still holding my arm. He said warmly, "Ralphie, you did a good job to-day when you captured Whitey Swenke. The bastard say why he did it?"

".Not to me, he didn't," I said.

"Well, it was a hell of a capture for a rookie trooper," Podre said.

"It was nothing. I fell into it."

" Never mind. You're a sharp kid and you were on the ball. And I don't blame you for picking up this boy. But no club doing any kind of business would throw away its licence by serving minors. The percentage isn't there, Ralphie."

" I guess not," I said. " I'm sorry I came in and kicked up a fuss, Carl."

" Forget it," Podre said. " What do you say I make a little announcement that you're the one who captured Swenke? These yokels will go big for it."

" Lay off that stuff. I'm not even supposed to be in here."

" Okay, okay," Podre said. " You come in on your time off. Old friends ought to get together. I mean it, kid. Anytime you have a chance, come in. Everything on the house."

" I'll see you, Carl." I began moving Cleves towards the door. I had seen Amy Bell approaching and I was anxious to get out. But before I could reach the door, she was at my side, her face laughing up at me, the black gown clinging to the slim curves of her body.

" Oh, good lord," she said. " Tell me, dear. Which juvenile is holding up which? "

I didn't answer her. Opening the door I brought Cleves outside.

When we reached the black Cadillac I asked the taffy-haired girl if she had a driver's licence. She did. Her name was Bonnie Chandler and her licence was in order. Then I asked the question I should have asked in the beginning. How did young Cleves get drunk? The girl explained that Cleves's father and mother had gone to a medical convention in New York and would not return until to-morrow. The boy had been staying with a family named Talbot. But young Cleves had a key to the house and a key to his father's liquor cabinet. His friend, Bob Talbot, had dared him to go home and open the cabinet. Dares to seventeen-year-olds are like red flags to a bull.

After young Cleves had become thoroughly drunk on his father's liquor he had driven over to Bonnie Chandler's house in his father's car. He had tooted the horn and Bonnie had come out. When she saw how drunk he was she didn't want her parents to see him. She thought she would drive him around until he sobered up. While driving they both got the idea of visiting Dorset to look at the murder scene. After they saw the house they drove through the square. Cleves noticed The Red Wheel and insisted on going inside.

" Who was doing the driving? " I asked.

" I was," she said. " And when we got into The Red Wheel I told the bartender Dickie was only seventeen. They put us out." She plucked at my sleeve. " Don't lock him up, please. I swear he's never done anything like this before. It was Bob Talbot who dared him. Otherwise Dickie would never have touched the stuff."

" I have to know what will happen if I turn him loose."

" Nothing will happen to him. I'll drive him straight to my house. My folks will take care of him. We're very close friends of the Cleveses."

I made a note in my book. " Get him out of here quick."

" Yes, sir," she said. " Thank you, sir."

I helped put Cleves in the car. " Take him straight home."

"Thank you very much," she said. She ran around to the driver's side of the big Cadillac, got in and started the motor. The headlights went on and she drove off.

I turned and started back across the road. As I did, I saw that Keith Ludwell was no longer in the diner. He was outside, standing beside the cruiser watching me.

"What happened?" he asked as I came up.

"Nothing much," I said. "A seventeen-year-old drunk. I sent him home."

"I noticed you went off the air."

So he had seen that the radio was shut off. Which meant he had been outside longer than I had thought.

"Yes," I said. "I sent in a 4."

His mouth pursed. "You shouldn't have. Not at midnight. When you signal 'off the air' at midnight, the dispatcher is liable to think we both left the cruiser and went in to eat together. It doesn't look good on the log."

I was just about sick of the whole business then and I almost opened my mouth to tell Ludwell so. I also wanted to tell him that he might be senior man and all that, and it was his job to correct me when I was wrong, but he sure was damn petty and picky about trivial things.

I didn't say anything, though. Opening the door I started to get into the cruiser.

"Aren't you going in for chow?" he asked.

"I'm not hungry," I said, a bit sullenly.

He looked at me, frowned, and got in behind the wheel. He gave the dispatcher a Signal 5 that we were back on the air and we rode out on patrol.

CHAPTER FOUR

OUR PATROL ended at three in the morning. When we arrived at the barracks I could see newspaper men hanging around outside. Corporal Phil Kerrigan was in the duty office and he logged us in. Then he told me I was wanted in the guardroom.

The room held an acrid blue mist of cigarette smoke, the stale odour of cigars. The floor that had been so carefully waxed and polished that morning was now scuffed and dirty. Around the long report table were a number of men in civilian clothes. I knew only one of them, State Police Detective-Lieutenant Sam Gahagan. He called me over and introduced me to the others. One of them was an assistant district attorney of Essex County, two were Boston detectives, one was a New York detective who had flown down that evening. The last one was Chief of Police Allen Rigsby of Dorset.

I was glad to see Rigsby there. Some big city cops have a mistaken idea about small-town police. Rigsby was a young man with calloused, oil-stained hands who owned an auto repair shop in Dorset. He received twelve hundred dollars a year for acting as the entire Dorset police department. He had no police car, no short-wave radio or teletype, no jail. He did not work full time at his police job because outside of a few legal papers to serve, town ordinances, an occasional town drunk, a rare theft, or pranksters, there wasn't much crime in Dorset. But what was important was that Rigsby knew every person in town, their character and disposition—far more than the townspeople realised. Also, he could spot a stranger in town. The fact that he had never seen Whitey Swenke was pretty good evidence that Swenke had not been in the centre of Dorset before.

The men around the [table looked very tired. Slumped in their chairs they kept sipping at cups of coffee, continually smoking. Gahagan asked me to repeat the part I had played in the capture of Swenke. Then he asked what, if anything, Swenke had said to me.

I told them.

" It's not much," Gahagan said, chewing on the stub of a soggy cigar. " But we haven't done any better with him. He's in the cellblock sleeping like a baby and we're all pooped out. So Swenke told you the story about another blue truck, did he? "

" Yes, Lieutenant," I said.

" It's an old worn-out tactic," Gahagan said. " He'll keep hammering about that mythical truck hoping some juror will have a doubt and think maybe there *was* another truck. The man was caught red-handed and that's the only story he can pull." Gahagan looked at his cigar with distaste and put it into an ashtray. " You had custody of Swenke's .38 automatic until Ballistics took it off your hands this afternoon, didn't you? "

" Yes, Lieutenant."

" The tests show that gun killed Mary Ann Fedder. We have five eyewitnesses who can describe Swenke. I'm afraid our friend Swenke is sewed in a bag."

" Is he going to be kept here long, Lieutenant? "

" No, he's already been photoed and printed. In

the morning we'll take him down to the Salem District
Court and arraign him for murder. He'll stay in the
county jail there until the trial. Our New York
friend," Gahagan said, gesturing to the New York
detective, " has some old scores to settle and he'd like
to fry Swenke in the chair at Sing Sing. But I think
we'll do the job for them." He rubbed the back of his
neck. " I wish that was the end of it. It isn't. Now
we have to go to work."

" Sir? " I asked.

" We've sent out a File 13 with his fingerprint
classification. We may have some more news about him
from other parts of the country. But we want to know
what he was doing in Dorset. The D.A.'s disturbed,
the whole town of Dorset is jittery. We can't think of
any kind of motive Swenke could have had for killing
this girl. We thought maybe she scraped fenders with
him on the road and he got mad at her. But there was
no damage to either car or truck. No, there must be
another reason why this professional killer showed up
around here, and we have to find out what it is."
Gahagan sighed wearily. " It's going to take a hell of a
lot of manpower. We've got to check this girl's life
back to the day she was born. We've got to check
the family, the boy friend, the neighbours, the school.
We've got to find out how long Swenke's been in
Massachusetts, where he's been staying, who he's been
seen with, why he went to the trouble of renting a truck.
We'll have to shake down every stool-pigeon we have.
I'd love to get Swenke into G.H.Q. and strap him to the
lie detector. He's refused to take it, of course."

The assistant district attorney was a grey-haired
man with rimless glasses. He said, " Lindsey, you did

a fine job in capturing Swenke." Then he smiled a little diffidently. " I think it was good you didn't know who he was when you grabbed him."

" Yes, sir," I said. " I'd have been a lot more nervous and a lot more trigger happy."

They all smiled tiredly. Gahagan said, " Well, Ralph, as arresting officer, you might as well put your own two cents in. Do you have any ideas on the subject? "

" Just one thing, Lieutenant," I said. " A man like Swenke might have a family somewhere. He might have written home and told them something. If we could find out where——"

Gahagan nodded. " Swenke has a mother in East Orange, New Jersey. She's coming to Salem to-morrow. But our New York friend says we shouldn't hope too much that she'll tell us anything."

The New York detective snubbed out his cigarette. " If she does, it'll be only by accident. That's why we try to talk to them as long as we can. Sometimes a word will slip out by mistake."

Gahagan said, " I'd talk her deaf, blind and dumb if I thought I could get a word out of her."

The New York detective smiled. He had a shrewd, rough-hewn face. " I know Swenke's old lady. You won't get much out of her. She's one of these quiet, patient mothers who thinks the whole world misunderstands her boy. She'll tell you about the pet dog he loved and the box of candy he always sends on Mother's Day. What happened to Whitey is the fault of cops picking on him and nasty people making up terrible stories about him. He was always good to his dog and his mother. And you might as well face it, Sam. Swenke is a psycho. He could have murdered this girl for a very small reason. He's a skilful killer, so sure of himself that there was no question in his mind he'd get away with it."

The assistant district attorney said, " Lindsey, how long have you been stationed here? "

" They just transferred me from the Concord Barracks, sir. I've been around only five days."

" What do you know about that Newburyport bank robbery three weeks ago? "

" Not much, sir. I was part of a roadblock on Route 2 near Acton. That was a long way from the scene, and the only part I played in it."

" Well," Lieutenant Gahagan said, " it's just an idea we had, Ralph. This was a hundred-thousand dollar robbery and the biggest score pulled in this area since the Danvers case. It was a well-planned job with only one little hitch. A Newburyport police officer who was supposed to have been at lunch was delayed by a little rear-end auto collision on Water Street. He wasn't too far away when the bank robbers came out of the bank. There were three of them, two for the stickup and one in the getaway car. The cop opened fire. One of the men slipped or fell, but was dragged into the car. The men were all masked and we had poor descriptions of them. Somehow the car—a stolen one—got through our roadblocks and was found abandoned in Everett two days later. There was never any report on a wounded man. Yet the Newburyport cop thinks he hit somebody."

" Not Swenke, Lieutenant? "

" No," Gahagan said. " You saw Swenke stripped. Did he look like he had been wounded a couple of weeks ago? "

" No, sir."

" So it wasn't Swenke. Yet Swenke is the type who'd hire himself out for a job of this kind. Also, here we find him in Dorset, which isn't too far from Newbury-port. Maybe there's a connection and maybe there isn't."

One of the Boston detectives said, " Lindsey, you know we're looking for man a named Hozak, don't you? "

" Yes, sir," I said. " George ' Slicker ' Hozak. There's been a general alarm out on him since the robbery."

" He's dropped out of sight since the bank stickup," the Boston detective said. " I still say this robbery was a typical, well-planned Hozak job. And I think there's a good chance Hozak hired Swenke as a gun."

Gahagan smiled grimly. " Marty, if Swenke was hired for the Newburyport job he should have been paid off and long gone. So now tell me what Swenke was doing here three weeks later in a rented truck, and why he killed the girl."

The Boston detective grinned wearily. " Sam, I've got enough troubles of my own."

I had a cup of coffee with them and they asked me again about the capture, laying particular stress on the route the truck had taken and following it on the wall map. I could sense frustration in them, because, although they had the murderer, they might never learn the reason why Mary Ann Fedder was killed.

I went back to the duty office to talk with Corporal Kerrigan, unbuckling my gunbelt, yawning a little because it had been a very long day. I explained to

Kerrigan about the Cleves boy. After the Fedder murder it all seemed very inconsequential. Yet it bothered me that perhaps I hadn't handled it correctly.

Kerrigan's eyes showed a great deal of interest. He said, " If I were you, Ralph, I wouldn't have made the decision myself. I'd have called Ludwell out of the diner."

" Dammit, why? " I asked. " I spent three months at the Academy. It was tougher than any basic training I had in the Army. I graduate and I'm sent to two other barracks for seasoning before I come here. Haven't I had enough training and background? By now I should be able to make my own decision on a minor drunk case, Phil."

" I should hope so," Kerrigan said. " But first you should have been sure you were on safe ground. Ludwell would have told you. You didn't ask him and now you've got some doubts about it. Because if you didn't have any doubts you wouldn't be asking me."

" Okay," I said. " So I should have called Ludwell. What else did I do that was so wrong? "

" You made a mistake going into The Red Wheel without all the information. If you'd questioned the girl she'd have told you they didn't serve young Cleves in The Red Wheel. Then you wouldn't have made a damn fool of yourself in there."

" All right," I said. " That was a mistake and I admit it. I'll be more careful from now on. And I'm glad to see the end of that one."

Kerrigan shook his head slowly. " You haven't seen the end of it, Ralph. There has to be a follow-through."

" Why? "

" The boy was drunk. If he gets away with drunkenness he might try it again. The State Police can't be a party to the concealment of it from a minor's parents. They have to be notified, Ralph. You understand why, don't you? Because if we don't, this Cleves kid will think he can do it again without the cops bothering him. Next time he might get involved in an accident and an innocent person might be killed. What then? Evidence will be shown that this kid was drunk before, that the police knew about it and neglected to notify the parents so they could take proper action. You'd get it in the neck, Ralph."

" I never figured I had to be a wet nurse for parents."

" So you've learned something to-night. Parents have a right to know about their own kid. You say they'll be back from New York to-morrow? "

" Yes."

" I'll phone them to-morrow evening myself," Kerrigan said. " But first we'll check the kid's name through to see if he has a record. Did you think of that? "

" That's one reason I walked in here," I said. " Good night, Phil, and thanks."

I left the duty office and went upstairs to my room. Ludwell was fast asleep in his bed near the window. I undressed in the dark and walked down the hall in my wooden clogs to take my shower.

I was thinking that would close the Cleves incident. After all it was pretty small stuff. Certainly it was nothing over which anybody would want to make an issue.

As it turned out, I was wrong.

CHAPTER FIVE

WHEN I GOT UP at ten that morning, Trooper Keith Ludwell was gone from the room. Along with four other experienced troopers in plain-clothes, he had been put on special assignment on the Fedder case. They told me Ludwell had left the barracks at nine in a black cruiser. Earlier, Kurt Swenke, heavily manacled and guarded, had been taken to Salem, arraigned for the murder and lodged in the county jail there. Now the cellblock and the guardroom of the barracks were cleaned and polished again, and the gardener-custodian had quit his mumbling and had gone back to his favourite mission—the front lawn.

It was one of those soft spring mornings, with a gentle breeze blowing from the west. Everything outside seemed to be bursting into flower. Next to the barracks, beyond an old stone wall, was an ancient Colonial cemetery which was preserved by some historical society. I could see workmen in there, grooming the grounds, getting them ready for the Memorial Day exercises.

Because I had been on a late patrol and my senior man was out, Sergeant Neal put me on barracks duty until noon. In fatigue clothes I washed and polished Cruiser 27, then worked on my reports.

Just before lunch Captain Roger Dondera, the troop commander, came down from Framingham. With him, to supervise the detectives in the investigation, was Detective-Lieutenant Edward Newpole from State

Police G.H.Q. in Boston. I knew Lieutenant Newpole well. He was an old family friend and I had worked with him on two other cases.

They called me into the guardroom and Newpole told me Swenke had been bound over for the grand jury and as arresting officer I would probably be called. He also told me that a well-known criminal lawyer had made a sudden appearance to take on Swenke's case.

Also, Mrs. Ilge Swenke, the widowed mother of Kurt, had arrived from New Jersey to see her son. She talked freely to the police and newspaper men. She said everybody was wrong, of course. Her son would not kill any harmless girl like Mary Ann Fedder. It was the usual frame-up and persecution of her son. Also her Kurt had been senselessly and brutally beaten over the head by the arresting trooper. She would look into the laws about prosecuting said trooper.

" She really believes all that? " I asked.

" Why not? " Newpole said. " She'll believe anything her boy tells her. Almost all mothers do. Mothers are the biggest suckers in the world when it comes to their own kids."

Two interesting points had come up in her interview with the police. Over a month ago she had received a postcard from Kurt postmarked Ipswich, Mass., and telling her about the famous clams he had eaten there. The Boston address on the automobile licence had been false and Swenke had not lived there. But the information about the postcard had sent state detectives scurrying to the Ipswich, Essex, Hamilton area. Ipswich was less than fifteen miles south of Newburyport and only a half-hour's ride from Dorset.

And if Swenke had been in Massachusetts over a month ago, he could have taken part in the Newburyport robbery.

No, she had not saved the postcard. Police always had a way of misinterpreting things. But she did remember, proudly, that her son had mentioned he was friendly with a priest. This raised some eyebrows because the last time Whitey Swenke had been near a priest was when he was fourteen and had committed a theft from a poor box in a church in New Jersey. Still the detectives would doggedly check all parishes for information.

There was one more bit of news. Mr. Fedder, the father of Mary Ann, had suffered a severe heart attack and was now at the Anna Jaques Hospital.

" It's too bad," I said when Newpole told me that. " They were more concerned about the mother."

" The father kept it in too long," Newpole said. " He had no safety valve like the mother. Their daughter was an only child. Naturally they tried to do all they could for her. The father wasn't a rich man. He was superintendent of some department in that big distillery in Newburyport." Newpole's face hardened. " Every time something new comes up it focuses on either Newburyport or Ipswich. I'm sending detectives all through the North Shore. So what do we expect to find? "

" Well," Captain Dondera said, " you sure as hell don't crack a case by sitting in an office drawing doodles on a scratch pad."

" Roger, you were smart to stay in the uniformed branch," Newpole said to him. " If I had to do it over, I'd be what you are."

" Not now," Dondera said, smiling broadly. " You're a little too old, Ed."

" I'd last forever on your job," Newpole said. " Your biggest worry is traffic on Route 128."

Dondera laughed. " You try running a troop and five sub-stations. It's ulcer stuff."

" Funny, I've got the ulcer," Newpole said, " not you."

" Sir," I said to Newpole, " how's the girl's fiancé taking it? "

" Russell Westlake? After the first shock wore off, he began to get damn mad. I wouldn't be surprised if he grabbed a shotgun and made for the Salem jail where Swenke has set up housekeeping. And I guess he's sore at the cops, too."

" Why the cops, sir? "

" We have to ask certain questions, Ralph. Was Mary Ann as innocent as they say? Did she ever meet Swenke before? Did she have an affair with him? Was Swenke jealous because she was marrying some-body else? Was her killing the result of a revenge motive? What did Westlake have to do with it? Did he have any reason to hire somebody to kill his girl? Those are all nasty questions, Ralph, but they have to be asked. Westlake got damn mad. If it was me, I'd have been mad, too."

" Yes, sir," I said. " It's only natural."

" We've cleared up the sex angle," Newpole said. " The autopsy shows Mary Ann wasn't attacked and she wasn't pregnant. In fact, she was a virgin. Unusual in this day and age, huh? "

" Ed, you're a cynic," Dondera said.

" I'm a realist," Newpole said. " What I want to

find out is what happened just prior to the murder. We know Mary Ann was driving into Dorset from the east, from the direction of Ipswich. Swenke was following her. After he killed her he didn't turn around. He kept heading west until Lindsey grabbed him. Usually, on a job, a careful criminal like Swenke maps a getaway route. If his plan was to travel west, where was he heading? Then take Mary Ann. The last we know anyone saw her was around noon. She had lunch with a girl friend named Rodna Dryden at Rodna's house on Elm Street. Mary Fedder left there at 12.30. She was in bubbling spirits and the two girls laughed a lot during lunch. When Mary Ann left, Rodna asked her where she was going. Mary Ann told her it was a big secret. But nobody knows what the secret was. Rodna reminded her there was a church rehearsal at 2.30. Mary said she'd be there. She drove off in her little Nash and that's the last anybody saw of her until two o'clock when she was killed. That gives us an hour and a half that's unaccounted for. What happened in that hour and a half that made Swenke chase her down and kill her? And where did it start? "

He looked at Captain Dondera, but Dondera was silent. Newpole shook his head and said, " We've questioned Swenke for hours. All we've got out of him is the story of the other blue truck. He's repeated it so long he's starting to believe it himself. Well, I'm going to ask our boy here." Newpole turned and eyed me. " Ralph, I want you to think back to Swenke's conduct when you were chasing him. Did he act like he knew where he was going? "

" I don't think he did," I said. "Not on 110. He

was swerving all over the road. He didn't know the turns. That's why I caught up with him so soon."

Newpole rubbed his nose. "I don't see it. He wouldn't kill the girl on the spur of the moment. He's not the type who loses his head. To him it's a job. He kills for money. This girl didn't have any money. Now—was it planned, or wasn't it?"

"It depends on how much time he had to plan," Dondera said. "It was done in broad daylight, in plain sight of witnesses. I know Swenke is supposed to be a big operator and sure of himself. But still, to me, the man was taking a big risk. The only thing I can say it must have come up suddenly. That forced Swenke to take the chance he did."

"I'll buy that," Newpole said. "He didn't chase her to see the colour of her pretty blue eyes. But what was it that came up so suddenly? And what was the packed suitcase doing in her car?"

"A suitcase, sir?" I asked.

"Filled with her clothes," Newpole said. "Maybe that was her secret. For all I know she might have been running off with Swenke, then changed her mind at the last minute. He got sore and killed her. If I knew more about women I'd say Swenke was definitely not her type. But who can tell what a woman will do?"

Nobody answered the question because I guess there was no answer to it. The two of them sat there silently for a few moments; then Captain Dondera looked up as though surprised I was still there. He dismissed me.

After lunch I got into uniform and took Cruiser 27 out. I had only a short patrol because I was going on a night pass at five. My territory was west of Dorset again, Route 110 and Pond Road. They ran parallel for several miles. I was to cover the sector to the Georgetown line.

But this time it wasn't a routine traffic patrol. I was carrying a picture of Kurt Swenke and I was to ask every store and house along the way if they had ever seen him. I knew troopers and detectives were in other areas, in Dorset and Newburyport and Ipswich, going from relative to friend, neighbour to neighbour and store to store. Old schoolmates and boy friends of Mary Ann were being questioned. In Boston, detectives would be at Simmons College and at the dormitories on Kent Street. Did Mary Ann Fedder ever go out with any men? Was there ever a time when she went out alone in the evening? Did any man ever call for her? Did she like a drink and a good time? Could she have possibly met a hoodlum like Kurt Swenke? Then— holding up a picture of Swenke—have you ever seen this man?

I drove through Dorset on my way out. In the town I spotted several black cruisers. Beyond the town I came to jumbled stone walls along the road and scattered, weather-beaten farmhouses set among gently rolling hills and rocky pastures.

I began to work—eagerly at first. A number of people along the route knew Mary Ann and were church members with her. Everybody had a kind word and an eulogy. Some had wild theories as to why the crime was committed. One old spinster said it was caused by the inherent bestiality of lust-maddened men. And she looked at me as though she didn't quite trust me either. But the more I went from residence to gas station to farm, the more my enthusiasm cooled. Most people talked too much and said the same thing. Some expressed shock and pious indignation, yet their eyes fastened on me greedily in the hope I had some juicy morsel to tell them. Nobody had seen Kurt Swenke or the blue panel truck.

I worked along steadily, reporting my locations to the dispatcher in Framingham. At 3.30 I was at the end of my sector. This was Pond Road as it curved and ended along Dorset Pond. Up ahead where the road ended were only some unoccupied summer camps.

The last house was set back from the road. It was not really a house but a converted summer cabin. The mailbox in front said, in faded letters, *Derechy*. As I stepped out of the cruiser I gave a dispatcher my location and a Signal 4.

I walked up a narrow, rutted dirt driveway. Parked in front of the house was a battered, decrepit old Hudson. The yard was piled with rubbish and garbage, a broken swing and broken, rusted toys. There was a fetid, rotting odour about the place. I banged on the front door.

The woman who opened it was young, but fat and slatternly. She wore a filthy housedress. Her dirt-encrusted feet were bare. There was a bad stench coming from inside the house.

" Hello," I said. " You're Mrs. Derechy? "

" Yes," she simpered.

I showed the Swenke picture. " Have you ever seen this man? "

She shook her head and burped. I could smell the sour odour of beer. Behind her, clutching at her dress,

were two tots about three and five. The three-year-old
was a boy, and the five-year-old was a girl. I knew
their sex because the only clothes they wore were short,
grimy, stained undershirts. Beyond Mrs. Derechy, on
a table in the middle of the room, were a dozen beer
cans. Sitting at the table was a fat, hairy, unshaven
young man with a puffy, drink-red face and unkempt
hair. He wore a dirty striped jersey and pants.

He said, " What the hell is it? "

I stepped around the litter on the floor, noticing
that the little girl had a red, running nose and little
scabby sores on her face.

" You're Mr. Derechy? " I asked the man.

" I'm not his mother," Derechy said. " What have
you got there? "

" A picture. I want to know if you've ever seen this
man."

Derechy took the picture in his big paw. He squinted,
studied it, held it up to the light. " What's the guy
done? "

" I want to know if you've ever seen him, that's all."

" Never in my life," he said. " Grace, this guy in
the picture a lover of yours? "

" Joe," Mrs. Derechy giggled coyly, " honestly, how
you carry on."

" My wife don't know him either," Derechy said.
" Anything else, trooper? "

I waved in the direction of the pond. " Any other
houses around here? I mean, where people are living? "

" About a half-mile down in Georgetown there's the
Fisher Farm. The rest of the places around here are
summer camps. They're all empty."

" All of them? "

" Wouldn't I know? I go all through there picking wood. It's as dead as a morgue. Be another month yet before any people start moving in."

" Ever see any cars ride by here? " I asked.

" Not during this time of year. At night, once in a while, the kids come along and park at the pond."

" Have you seen a blue panel truck? "

" No."

" One of those little baby Nash cars? "

" Ain't seen it. You don't see nothing go by here during the day."

" Notice anything strange lately? "

" No, nothing. What's this, the Mary Ann Fedder murder? "

" That's right," I said.

" I don't know nothing about it. I got my own troubles. Anything else? "

" No, that's all," I said, turning to go. " Thanks."

" Don't thank me, trooper. Just take the air, boy."

I turned around and moved up to him. " What's the matter, Derechy? You itching for trouble? "

He stared at me for a moment, his lips pouting. Then his eyes dropped. " Trouble is all I ever get from you guys. You're always nosing around here poking in my business."

" Not me," I said. " And if I ever have to come here again it'll be with a clothes-pin clamped to my nose."

I walked out, down the driveway, gulping the sweet fresh air and feeling that I needed a bath. In the cruiser I gave a Signal 5. My calls were over.

A hundred yards below the Derechy house the road curved sharply as it met the shore of the pond. I drove down the road, following the turn. The road went over a rise to a small bluff. At the top of the bluff the road ended. Here the shoulders were wide because it was a turn-around.

I stopped the cruiser. The view was pretty. You caught the graceful, drooping willows that edged the pond below. There was a stretch of sandy beach and, beyond it, the sparkling blue water.

Apparently I wasn't the only one who thought it was a good parking spot. There were rusted beer cans, crumpled cigarette packs and candy wrappings. Across the rippling water, on the other side, I could see several small piers. And, scattered among the trees, I could catch a glimpse of a roof or a side of an occasional cottage. Up ahead of me, on my own side of the pond, where the road ended, a pair of dual dirt tracks descended the hill and disappeared into the woods. I saw, partly obscured by the pines, one summer camp whose windows seemed to be shuttered with steel boiler plating.

A blue-jay chattered nearby. It was so quiet and peaceful and fragrant I thought I would stay and have a cigarette. Before I realised it I had been there a half-hour. To tell the truth, if I could have taken the chance of not being spotted, I might have slipped off my uniform and gone in for a swim. I don't know if Keith Ludwell would have. I rather think he wouldn't. But I never pretended to be as eager as Keith Ludwell.

As I sat there I wasn't thinking of the Mary Ann Fedder case. I was visualising Amy Bell. The truth was she had been sneaking into my mind all day and I had been pushing her away. I don't know why I persisted in thinking about her. She had never shown the slightest interest in me except annoyance. But she was attractive and desirable and sophisticated and there's something of a mysterious allure that an older girl has when you're not too many years past twenty-one.

I did more than think about her. I made plans to see her.

CHAPTER SIX

I WAS BACK in the barracks at four-thirty. Tony Pellegrini was in the garage when I pulled in. He was in fatigue clothes and was washing his cruiser. We spoke a few moments and he gave me some additional bits of information about the Fedder case. Then he said, " The joint is still hopping with brass. I guess they want to see you in the guardroom. The Westlake kid is there."

I went up the stairs and into the guardroom. Mary Ann Fedder's fiancé was seated at the long table. He was a tall, thin, snub-nosed, good-looking kid of about twenty-two, with a pale, harried face. His eyes were red as though he had been crying. Lieutenants Newpole and Gahagan were seated opposite him. At the end of the table was Chief Rigsby of Dorset. Newpole waved me over.

He introduced me to Russell Westlake, then said, " Russell, this is the man you wanted to see. Lindsey was the arresting officer."

Westlake looked at me intently, then said, " You want to know *why* I asked to see you? "

"Why, yes," I said. "If there's anything I can do——"

"I want to know why you didn't kill Swenke."

"I'm not sure I understand you——" I started to say.

"I said I wanted to know why you didn't kill Swenke."

"I don't know if you're serious," I said. "But we have courts and laws. You don't deliberately kill a man no matter what he's——"

"*I'd* have killed him," Westlake said, his voice keening. "I'd kill him now if I could get near him. I don't care what they'd do to me."

Lieutenant Newpole said mildly, "We wouldn't have much law and order that way, would we?"

"Law and order?" Westlake blurted out. "What the hell kind of law and order *do* we have? Why did a known killer, scum like Whitey Swenke, walk around free? What did the police ever do about him? Nothing. He comes to Dorset as free as a bird. He feels like killing a girl and he does it."

"Swenke has done time before," Lieutenant Sam Gahagan said. "Long stretches of it. And you should understand this, Russell. Criminals like Swenke are cannibalistic. They live off each other, robbing, stealing and murdering mostly among themselves. It isn't always easy to get evidence of those kind of homicides. When New York finally did get evidence on Swenke, he went on the run. This time we have him, Russ."

"The fact that you caught him doesn't bring Mary Ann back to life. He should never have had the opportunity."

I think Westlake had a point there and I, for one, wouldn't argue it. Now he was looking at me as though he had expended all his ammunition on the others and I was a new traget.

" You're my age, Lindsey," he said bitterly. " You're probably thinking of getting married. I'll sell you a gold wedding band real cheap."

" Take it easy, kid," Newpole said gently.

" Don't tell me to take it easy," Westlake said. " The cops come around asking insinuating questions about Mary Ann. They're not interested in finding out why she was killed. All they want to do is dig up some dirt for those reporters outside."

" Now, Russ, you really don't mean that——" Chief Rigsby started to say.

" If you were on the job, you'd make Swenke talk. I know *I* could make him talk."

Newpole's jaw became rigid. " What do you suggest, Russell? The Chinese water torture? Or hot pincers under the fingernails? "

" Very funny," Westlake said. " Very, very funny."

" It's not funny at all," Newpole said, " and that's why you have no cause to talk foolish."

" Now I know where I stand," Westlake said ominously. " I'll handle it my own way. I can do things the cops can't do."

Newpole looked over at me with one of those dismissal glances. I excused myself and left.

I reported to Sergeant Neal in the duty office. Neal asked me if I had obtained any information on my calls. I told him I had not. Then I mentioned my experience with the Derechys.

Neal's shoulders drooped tiredly. "Those damn Derechys again. How did the house look? Like a pigsty?"

"Worse."

"And the two kids?"

"Filthy."

Neal drummed his fingers on the desk. "We've had the S.P.C.C. and the Welfare and our own police-women there time and time again. This Derechy has a record. He's a lazy, drunken troublemaker, and he costs the Commonwealth plenty because he won't support his family. We've had those two up for child neglect so many times it became monotonous. You always get a soft-hearted judge who talks of mother love. Boloney. Those kids would be better off in a clean, decent foster home. They'd have a chance then. This Grace Derechy is a stupid, drunken, dirty woman. Let her husband beat her and starve her and she still thinks he's a Clark Gable and an Einstein all rolled into one. One of these days those kids will die of disease or get burned up in a fire caused by a drunken brawl. But you can't spoil the sanctity of the home." He made an entry in the log-book. "You going on a night off now?"

"Yes, Sarge," I said.

Neal leaned forward on the desk. I noticed his light blue uniform shirt was tight at the seams. Some sergeants, when they are promoted from the activity of patrol work to the desk, have a tendency to put on weight. Especially those who make frequent trips to the convenient kitchen. He said, "How are you getting along with Ludwell?"

"Fine."

" You'll learn a lot from Keith. He knows his stuff and he's a lot of help to me here. Some of the boys around here say he's a shaper. I don't see anything wrong with a man being a shaper. I *want* my men to be shapers—but good shapers. Understand? "

" Yes, Sarge."

" I always say look in the mirror before you go out on patrol. Your reflection is the public's impression. I like the way Keith looks all the time. And I like the way he goes by the book. Sometimes a new boot thinks he can try short cuts. I know every short cut that's ever been tried. Don't do it, Ralph. Don't get careless and don't ever dog it on me."

" I'll try not to."

" You dogged it to-day. Don't do it again, Ralph."

I felt my face flush. " When was that Sergeant? "

Neal said coldly, " You had the Pond Road patrol. You gave us a Signal 5 at 3.30. That was from the Derechy house. Where did you go then? "

" Continued on patrol until I came to the pond."

" Sure. I don't need any spies. I know every inch of this territory and I know exactly what you did. You came up the hill to the bluff. The hard road ends there. All you have after that are a couple of dirt tracks along the pond. You didn't drive up those tracks, did you? "

" No, I didn't."

" Your book doesn't show any violation slips after that. So unless you were parked up on that bluff for a half-hour, where the hell else were you? "

" I guess I was parked on the bluff, Sergeant."

" Did you go in for a swim? "

" No, I didn't."

" Maybe you didn't. In my time I've ridden patrol

there and I've sneaked a swim, too. So any trick you think you're pulling has been pulled before. Don't try to fool us, Ralph. You'll wind up behind the eight ball."

" I won't try it again."

" Keep it clean. Don't get a big head because you've made a lucky pinch, and maybe, some day, you'll be a good trooper. You going home now? "

" Yes, I am."

" Give my regards to your father. Any time you feel you can bring him out here, I'd like him to have lunch with us."

" Thanks, I'll tell him, Sergeant."

I went upstairs to my bare, austere room, undressed, showered and changed to civilian clothes. I had a short-barrelled S. & W. revolver which I used as my pocket weapon when I went off duty. I put it in the little holster and strapped it to the side of my belt. Then I went downstairs again to the parking lot. As I passed the garage I saw Pellegrini finishing up with his cruiser. I went over to him.

" Tony," I said, " what's your definition of a ' shaper ' ? "

He squeezed water from a cloth and eyed me curiously. " What's the matter, kid? You've heard the word before."

" Sure," I said. " I've heard talk. But I've never seen one."

" They're rare birds," Pellegrini said, leaning against the car. " You have to look close for them. A shaper is a bandbox, a trooper who's extra sharp about his appearance. He uses Simonize on his boots and usually carries a polishing cloth in his pocket. He's not satisfied with the fit the troop tailor gave his uniform, but has it recut to give it extra flair. Some of them have their silver uniform buttons dipped in chrome finish."

" I don't see anything wrong with that, Tony," I said. " I've done some of those things myself. The Division is always after us about being proud of the uniform."

" Who says it's wrong? " Pellegrini said, putting the cloth down. " ' Shaping up ' is good if it ends there. This is a semi-military outfit and smart-looking troopers are important. In fact, this is the most *military* semi-military outfit I've ever seen, and I've done my share of soldiering, so I know. But I'll tell you when it gets bad, kid. It gets bad when the uniform becomes more important than the work. There's where your bad shaper comes in. He likes the authority and the prestige of the State Police uniform because it helps make a hit with the girls. And who suffers? All the other troopers. They take the abuse."

" How? " I asked.

" I'll tell you how," Pellegrini said. " You have two men riding patrol together. One of them is a shaper. Say there's an accident. The shaper leaves the dirty work to the other man while he struts up the road to divert traffic. When newsmen arrive he's the one who says he's in charge of the investigation, while his partner is grubbing through the wreck and making out reports. In motor violations the shaper is always looking for the big cars, especially if he sees a girl driving. His partner is given the trucks and small cars. A shaper always likes to stop where there are a lot of people around. That way they can seen him in action. You getting the picture now, Ralph? "

" It's coming to me." I grinned.

" Good," Pellegrini said. " You have to watch out for a shaper. He can be pretty tricky. He's the eager beaver of the barracks. I don't mind a guy being eager. I'm eager myself lots of times. Everybody's got to pitch in and help. But it's one thing to be helpful and another thing to offer your personal car to the sergeant when the sergeant goes on a day off. The shaper is always sucking up to the brass. He always manages to be around when the inspecting staff sergeant or lieutenant shows up. That's where he shines. He'll point out little flaws for the good of the service, dropping a hint here and there about all the good he could do if he had stripes on his sleeves. If he's a cut-throat shaper he'll hint that the corporal is doing a lousy job. Not that he has anything personal against the corporal, understand? He happens to like the corporal as a friend. But, for the good of the service, he could handle the job better."

" I've got it," I said. " Thanks, Tony."

" What made you ask me, kid? "

" Nothing."

Pellegrini nodded. " Anyway, I'm glad you asked me. To tell the truth, I was going to get around to giving you a briefing on shapers myself. Keep your eyes peeled for them, kid. They'll do you no good."

I left him and got into my '46 Ford coupé. I waved to Pellegrini, drove out on to Route 1 and headed south for Cambridge.

As I drove I was thinking of a shaper named Keith Ludwell. There had always been a lot of kidding about shapers, but we had had none at the Concord Barracks, nor at the barracks in the western part of the state. I had never seen one until I met Ludwell. I remembered now that, as far as Ludwell was concerned, there wasn't the usual warm comradeship at the Topsfield Barracks. The other troopers were friendly but a little distant to him. Yet not one of them had ever made a single derogatory remark to me about Ludwell. That was understandable, of course. A cop usually never talks against another cop. Rightly or wrongly, they have a certain clannish code about those things. You had to find out by yourself.

The trouble was, sometimes you found out about them a little too late.

CHAPTER SEVEN

I ARRIVED HOME in Cambridge in time for supper. My mother made her usual fuss over me and the usual remark that I was getting thinner, although I had gained two pounds.

My father was sitting quietly and patiently in his wheel-chair, his hands pale and blue-veined on the little coverlet. Beneath the coverlet were his useless, paralysed legs. Every time I came home my heart gave a little wrench because I could see he was failing and becoming more aged and haggard-looking.

Before supper I wheeled my father out on to the front porch. His eyes had a happy little glint in them as he said, "You made a good pinch yesterday, Ralph."

"Plain luck and you know it," I said, sitting down in the glider near him. "I happened to be out there on patrol, that's all."

"But you didn't fumble it," he said. "In a way, everything is luck, son. It was luck that you came home from Korea alive and Paul Podre was buried there."

I knew what else he was thinking. It was luck that he had been shot in the back by a drunken wife-beater when he was corporal at the Andover Barracks many years ago. With Trooper Ed Newpole, he had gone out to make an arrest. After my father had been shot down, Newpole, coming from the rear of the house, had killed the wife-beater. To-day Newpole was a detective-lieutenant and my father was a broken old man in a wheel-chair. It might have happened the other way around, depending on who had taken the front of the house and who had the back. That was luck, too.

"I met Carl Podre last night," I said. Then I told him about it.

My father's face grew thoughtful. "I'd keep away from Carl, if I were you. He's a wrong one. I had him tabbed as a wrong one a long time ago."

"I don't think he has a record," I said.

"He can't beat the odds forever. Keep away from him, Ralph."

"I don't intend to be friendly with him," I said. I wasn't lying about it. If I was planning to visit The Red Wheel again it wasn't because of Carl Podre. Amy Bell was there.

"How are they making out with the Fedder case?" my father asked.

" They'll get a conviction," I said. " Nobody is worried about that."

" But a conviction won't end it," my father said. " You've got to see a case like this all the way through. You just don't convict a hired gunman for killing a young girl and let it rest there. You have to dig in and find out what caused it, who was standing behind the curtain pulling the strings."

" They're working hard on it," I said. " So far they've run into a stone wall. The girl has no bad past. She was graduating as a physical education instructor at Simmons, and she was going to be married in two weeks. She was a quiet girl. No men in her life except Russell Westlake."

" What about him? "

" Nothing. No other girl friend. Nobody who could be jealous because he was marrying Mary Ann. He's as clean as a whistle. Twenty-two years old, graduated from Lowell Tech. last year and now working as an engineer in a cotton mill in Salem. Neither of them had much money. They were planning to live with the Fedders, and the girl was going to be a gym. instructor for a couple of years until they got a nest egg saved. Funny thing about the girl. I always pictured physical education instructors as being horse-faced, beefy women. Mary Fedder was small, blonde and pretty. And there's no way she could have met Whitey Swenke, either. Most of the year she was at school, and she never went out."

" She *did* meet him," my father said. " Otherwise he wouldn't have killed her. He didn't pick her name out of a hat." He looked thoughtfully down the street and ran a hand over his fine-spun grey hair.

"The question is how and where and why." His hands moved restlessly over the coverlet. "How had she been up to the time she was murdered? Happy?"

"Oh, yes. She was busy all morning with her wedding things. There was to be a church rehearsal in the afternoon. She had lunch with Rodna Dryden, one of her bridesmaids. The Dryden girl says that Mary Ann didn't seem to have a care in the world. She left the Dryden house at twelve-thirty. Well, you know the rest of it. She was murdered at two o'clock in her own house."

"In that hour and a half she may have met Swenke for the first time in her life. The farthest she could have been away from home is a three-quarters of an hour ride."

"Which takes in a lot of territory," I said.

"Isn't Ipswich less than three-quarters of an hour away?"

"Yes, Pa. They're checking all through there."

"And Swenke had chased her car. Why was he driving a rented truck?"

"We don't know. He got it in Boston earlier that day."

My father shook his head. "The girl must have witnessed something. The question is what?"

"There's no record of anything, Pa. It happened to be a quiet day for crime."

"Nothing in the Ipswich area?"

"Nothing anywhere. One gas station hold-up in Haverhill. But they were two young punks and were grabbed by the Haverhill police."

"No missing persons reported?"

"No. And another thing. The girl had a packed suitcase in her car. Go figure that out."

"It's a tough one," my father said, kneading his fingers. "You'll find Ed Newpole will do a good job, though. How do you like Topsfield?"

"Fine."

"It's liable to be a little noisy. The trucks coming down the hill on U.S. 1 backfire a lot. You'll have to get used to sleeping there."

"I sleep like a log," I said. "By the way, Sergeant Neal sends his regards. He'd like to have you come out for lunch some day."

"That's mighty nice of Neal," my father said. "Mighty nice. I've been a little tired lately. When I feel stronger I'll be glad if you'll drive me out, Ralph. I'd appreciate it very much."

"I'll be happy to do it, Pa. How would next week be?"

"I hope next week will be fine. You going out on a date to-night?"

"I've got some tentative plans."

"Anybody local?"

I shook my head. That was a tender subject between us. I had been engaged to Ellen Levesque, who lived only two houses away. At the last minute it hadn't worked out. Ellen was seeing somebody else these days.

"I just thought I'd ask," my father said. "Your mother doesn't like to keep harping on it, so she passes the buck to me. She was always very fond of Ellen."

"It wasn't in the cards," I said.

"No, I suppose not," he said. And just then my mother called us in to supper.

CHAPTER EIGHT

I WAS IN DORSET at ten in the evening. When I walked into The Red Wheel I saw the place was half-empty. The stage was bare. I didn't see Amy Bell and I began to think I had come back for nothing. It could be her night off, too.

I went into the taproom. The bartender recognised me and asked what I would have. I was never much for drinking so I told him I'd let him decide.

" I've got some good bonded bourbon," he said. " Private stock. It'll taste just right with a little soda."

" Fine."

He poured the drink into a small shot glass and set it beside a glass of soda with a single ice cube in it. " Mix it for you? "

" Please."

He mixed it with a swizzle stick. " I'm Harry," he said. " I've been here two years and been tending bar sixteen years altogether. And I'd like you to know I've never served a minor in my life. Not knowingly."

" I'm sorry about last night," I said. " I guess I got over-excited."

" It's not your fault," he said. " A cop can't be too careful. You must see a lot of that stuff going on."

" I haven't myself. But I've been told to watch out for it." I took a dollar bill from my wallet and placed it on the bar.

Harry pushed it back. " Orders," he said. " Carl said anything you want is on the house."

" Well, thanks," I said, looking dubiously at the dollar bill. " Does Carl treat all cops the same way? "

" Just Al Rigsby, the local gendarme. He doesn't come in here more than once a month and all he'll have is a bottle of beer."

" I mean state cops."

" You're the first trooper who ever came in here. Sometimes on a Friday or Saturday night there'll be a prowl car outside watching for drunken drivers. But none of them troopers ever come in here."

" I feel kind of funny being the exception."

" Forget it. Carl says you're an old friend of his. He tells me you went around with his kid brother who was killed in Korea."

" Yes, I did." I sipped on the bourbon. It was fiery going down.

" How's the drink? " Harry asked. " Good?' '

" Fine," I said. " Kind of quiet to-night, isn't it? "

" It's a little early yet," Harry said. " But I can tell it's going to be a slow night. Maybe it's the murder. The letdown comes afterwards. Last night there were a lot of townsfolks in here lapping it up, all excited, talking their heads off about it. To-day they must be feeling a little ashamed of themselves."

" That could be it," I said.

" You sure grabbed that killer fast," Harry said. " He put up a fight? "

" Not much."

" I've got to laugh. A gangster with a big rep. A real tough guy. But you give a hyena a gun and he thinks he's a lion. The guy must have been crazy, too. There's a killing that had absolutely no sense to it. I was telling that to the detective who was in here last night asking questions. I said there was absolutely no sense to it. That Mary Ann Fedder was a hell of a fine girl."

" You knew her? "

" No. But she come in here once to collect for a church bazaar. I sent her to Carl. You could see she was a good, clean girl. I'd like to throw the switch on Whitey Swenke myself. Those muscle guys I could never stand."

" Did Russell Westlake ever come in here? "

" The boy friend? No. Those kids don't come in here at all. They don't have the money to spend. They can have a good time by going down the road to the ice cream stand and buying a Coke or a box of fried clams."

I sipped on the bourbon. Harry ran a damp rag over the bar. He said, " Carl tells me you haven't been a trooper long. How do you like the State Police?"

" Fine," I said.

" Rugged, huh? Like the Army? "

" A lot stricter," I said. " But they make up for it in the pay. Isn't Amy Bell singing to-night? "

" Oh sure. She's around somewhere. Comes on later. Say, she's burned up at you, isn't she? "

" I didn't know."

" You booked her for speeding."

" That's all right. *I'm* not mad at her."

Harry laughed. " Why should you be? You gave out the ticket. Not her."

" What time does Amy go on? "

" In about half an hour. The girl sure draws a crowd here. The first time she came here was last spring. Stayed until the fall. Then she left to make a tour of different clubs. She came back last week for a three-week engagement. I guess she could earn a lot more dough elsewhere, but maybe she figures she owes something to Carl. He gave her her start, you know."

" No, I didn't know. Carl has a big club here."

" Sure. I don't think he actually owns much of it, though. Most of these clubs are controlled by outside people. Might be a half-dozen people each owning a piece of it for all I know. But Carl runs it."

" No back room? "

" Gambling? Here? Would I tell you if there was? " He laughed. " Naw, I was only kidding. No gambling. Couldn't get away with it if we tried. This is a tough spot for gambling."

" Carl's lucky to have Amy Bell singing here," I said.

Harry wiped the bar again. " You keep mentioning Amy Bell," he said, an odd little smile on his face. " Kind of like her? "

I grinned. " She's a hell of an attractive woman."

" Thanks, Daddy-o," a woman's voice said. I turned. Amy Bell was standing directly behind me.

She said, " I'm afraid it was a dirty trick. Harry saw me coming up to the bar and he asked you a loaded question."

I grinned again. " I still say you're a hell of an attractive woman."

Harry laughed, shook his head, moved away and began to mix a drink.

" I'm beginning to like you a little," Amy Bell said. " Let's go sit in a booth, dear. Harry's making my usual Tom Collins. I always have one before I start to work. Gin is kind to my throat. Must be the juniper in it."

We crossed the floor and sat down in a red-leather-padded booth. Harry brought over the Tom Collins and nudged me.

" Keep going, kid," he said. " You're doing good."

" I'm trying," I said.

" How about another bourbon?

" Let me nurse this one," I said.

He went away. I looked at Amy Bell, at the soft red mouth, the black, glossy, luxuriant hair, the roundness of her smooth face, the long eyelashes, the supple, catlike sensual body sheathed in a form-fitting black gown. There was an extra femaleness in her. Not femininity but femaleness—there seems to be a difference between the two.

" You like what you see? " she asked directly.

" I sure do," I said simply. " Why do you always wear black? "

" Good for business," she said. " Black is sexy. I also wear black lace panties, and when I go to bed it's a black chiffon sheer nightie. But to-night I'm absolutely bare under my evening gown. Not a stitch on, really."

" Don't try to startle me, honey," I said. " I'm a big boy now. My mother even lets me go to the barber shop myself these days."

She laughed in her throat. " You *are* a big boy, aren't you? " she said, her eyes wandering over me. " And I've been mean and nasty to you, haven't I? "

" Nobody ever treated me worse."

She smiled delicately. " But you came back for more, Daddy-o."

" I'm a glutton for punishment."

" Stubborn, stubborn," she said. " How old are you, anyway? "

" Twenty-three."

" A child," she said. " But I've been reading such wonderful things about you. All about the little David who captured the big, bad Goliath yesterday."

" The name is Ralph," I said. " And he was no Goliath. He was a lot smaller than I was."

" But you're only a child." She sighed. " Oh, what I'd give to be back to your age."

" You're not so far away from it."

" I'm all of twenty-five."

" Twenty-seven."

" That's the trouble with becoming friendly with a cop. You saw that damn driver's licence. Now I can't even snip two years off my age." She lifted her glass and drank. " Well, I'm still in the spinster classification."

" Only by choice," I said.

She toyed with her glass. " You always say the right things, don't you? They must give state troopers a terrific course in public relations. Why, you were so smooth and polite with that ticket last night, I thought I was being patriotic to my country by taking it. When I go in to court to pay the fine I'll probably salute the colours."

" It's like painless dentistry," I said. " We try to keep our customers happy."

" You've made me absolutely delirious," she said. " What's the next step in your plan of conquest, dear? "

" Now I get you to talk about yourself. That always breaks the ice."

" Aren't you going to tell me how gorgeous I am and where have I been all your life? "

I shook my head. " That's the old dance-hall line.

It went out with the horse car. The approach nowadays is more subtle."

She smiled and, surprisingly enough, she did begin to talk about herself. She had been born in Plainville, Connecticut, and had studied piano and voice in Hartford. A short term at the Boston Conservatory had convinced her that her voice was suitable for popular music and no more. Getting started was the hardest part. First there had been the amateur shows and benefits, any place where she could get a little recognition. It was Carl Podre who had given her her first professional booking. That was last summer. From her earnings she had made the down payment on the red convertible, registering it in Dorset where she had been staying. After some months at The Red Wheel she had acquired an agent, and he booked her into a small supper club in Chicago. Then it was Salt Lake City and Reno and Las Vegas and San Francisco. All small clubs, she explained, but you had to build up booking dates like credits. With each new club she got small increases in her contract. Now she was back at her first place, The Red Wheel. It wasn't altogether altruistic on her part. She was getting paid double what she had received last year.

" Then what? " I asked.

" The ultimate goal, of course, is New York. The big supper clubs. Along with those you hope for records, radio, TV, pictures. If you really want to dream, you hope for a show of your own or the lead in a big Broadway hit musical. That's about the peak. How many of us do you think ever reach it? "

" You will," I said. " I heard you sing last night."

"Thank you, Oscar Hammerstein," she said. "Do you have a cigarette, please?"

I took out my pack and lit a cigarette for her. She blew a thin wreath of blue smoke. I looked down at her left hand holding the glass. She noticed my glance.

"There's no marriage ring on that third finger, Sherlock Holmes," she said. "Which means, obviously, that I'm not married. Now don't be typical and ask me why."

"Why?" I asked.

"Now you've forced me to answer. No girl can resist talking about marriage." She inhaled slowly on the cigarette, her eyes focused distantly. "Marriage is a problem that haunts every girl who thinks she has a little talent. Which shall it be? Marriage or a career, or both? So far, for me, the career has come first."

"I'm curious about that," I said. "How do you ward off all the offers?"

"What kind?" she asked a little bitterly. "I get all kinds of offers. You'd be surprised at some of the shocking offers this little girl gets. One of these days some nice, young, clean-cut chap might even propose marriage. I hope I won't die from the surprise."

"I think you're acting a little too defensive about it. Maybe you've had honest offers and your own acceptance had a string dangling from it. Maybe the man who makes the offer has to have an orchid corsage in one hand and his bankbook in the other."

She smiled and shook her head. "Either, at your age, you've developed an old cop's analytical mind, or I must be as transparent as that fictitious chiffon nightie I mentioned. You're right, dear. I don't believe in love in a garret. That's for peasants."

" You may be wrong. Peasants are supposed to be happier than princes. Love is supposed to make the world go 'round. Didn't you ever hear bells ringing inside? "

" That's only a fairy tale, Junior. I've been around too long to swallow it. You see, I've come in contact with many men. There isn't one of them I'd want to bring home to Mother and say, ' Look what I caught, Mother dear.' Do I sound just a wee bit cynical to you? "

" Just mildly."

" It takes one to know one," she said. " The most cynical people in the world are cops." She sipped on her drink. " How long have you been a trooper? "

" Not very long."

" I knew it. You're still starry-eyed and wallowing around in idealism. Wait a few years, dear, and we'll compare notes brooding over our absinthe."

She was wrong, though. I had seen enough rottenness and sordidness in the world. I had been to Korea and seen war. And I had come in contact with all kinds of people in my short career as a police officer. The world would never be a Utopia. There would always be thieves, murderers, rapists and sadists. I knew all that. But I also knew you could control criminals, like you did insects and bacteria, so they were always in the minority.

And, of course, to bring it closer to home, it had to be Joe Derechy walking into the taproom just then.

He was wearing a pair of sloppy pants and a colourful, but dirty, sport shirt. He had shaved since I had seen him in the afternoon, but that didn't appear to

make him very much cleaner. It would have taken
six men with sand soap and steel brushes working
six hours to do that. His gait was unsteady and his
face was red with drink. With him were two men, both
sharp-faced, loudly dressed men who had the appearance of race-track touts. Derechy walked up to the bar,
pulled out a wad of crumpled bills, threw them on the
counter, then banged loudly for drinks.

I watched the reaction of Harry, the bartender.
There was a worried, wary look on his face. I was
puzzled, too. Derechy was not the type of clientele
that visited The Red Wheel. Not a man whose family
had been receiving welfare. But here he was at the
bar treating others to drinks.

Harry mixed the drinks slowly. When he brought
them, Derechy urged his two companions to drink,
acting very much like a big advertising account
executive hovering over important clients. The men
tasted their liquor, one bending over to Derechy and
whispering. Derechy guffawed and said something
obscene in a loud voice.

Harry moved in quickly. His mouth was pinched.
With a gesture of pained, polite caution he pointed to
the presence of Amy Bell in the booth.

Derechy turned, looked at the booth, then nudged
his friends. The three of them laughed uproariously.
I saw Harry begin to get a little fidgety as he peered
towards the entrance of the bar. I didn't know if The
Red Wheel had a bouncer, but this was more than
Harry could handle alone. I was debating whether
to move Amy Bell out when Derechy left the bar and
sauntered over to the booth.

He didn't recognise me in civilian clothes because he

said, " Hey, college boy, I've got the word on your friend. Watch out you don't get your fingers burnt with this song thrush. She's been around."

I looked quickly at Amy Bell and saw her hand clutching her glass so tightly that her knuckles turned white. There were tiny beads of moisture on her upper lip.

I said, " Derechy, why don't you go home and take care of your wife and kids? "

He squinted at me. Then his eyes widened. " Hey, the cop." He turned and waved for his two friends. They came up to the booth and he said, " See this young kid? He's a state trooper. Honest."

The two men smirked. One in a panama hat said, " Don't tell me, Joe. Not this nice little boy."

" On the level," Derechy said. " And a nosy sonova-bitch. The kind who comes barging into your house asking questions, then insults you."

The panama hat said, " Joe, I wouldn't let no cop insult me."

I stood up, squeezing by them, moving a few feet away from the booth, trying to draw them away from Amy Bell so she wouldn't get hurt. My heart was beating rapidly and my larynx felt squeezed tight. I said, " Get out of here, Derechy."

The panama hat edged closer to me. He had little black-agate eyes. He smiled softly. " I eat young cops for breakfast."

He was a small, runty bowlegged man and I didn't waste any time with him. I pushed him suddenly on the chest with the flat of my hand. He fell over backwards, bounced on the floor and started to slither away like a snake.

Derechy said to the other, " Come on, Augie. Let's take this kid."

He closed his big fist and brought his arm back. But I jammed my heel down hard on his instep. He bent, howling. As he did, I grabbed the upended seat of his pants and his collar. Pushing him ahead of me, I ran him across the floor, our momentum carrying us through the taproom entrance into the foyer. I opened the front door and hustled him outside into the parking lot. He was shouting to the other two for help, at the same time twisting to get at me. I hooked one leg under his and threw him to the ground. When he tried to get up I pushed him down with my foot.

" Stay there a moment," I said. " Breathe some of the cool night air."

The fight seemed to have gone out of him suddenly, because he sat there and started to sob.

The door of The Red Wheel opened and Derechy's two friends came out, their heads moving from side to side looking for us. Behind them I saw Harry standing anxiously in the doorway. I reached back for my pocket gun. I didn't have my billy with me but the butt of the S. & W. would do fine.

But nothing happened. Neither of the two men was interested. I looked at the man in the panama hat, but he bent his head and hurried to a car. The other followed him. They got in, started the car and drove off.

I turned back to Derechy and lifted him to his feet. " Your two friends drove off and left you," I said. " You could buy their drinks but not their help."

" Bastards," Derechy mumbled.

" Go on home before you get into more trouble."

" My car ain't here.'

" Walk."

" I've got important friends," he said. " We'll fix your wagon. You wait and see."

" Get out of here or I'll boot you all the way home."

He stumbled down the road, disappearing in the darkness. I went back inside The Red Wheel, going by Harry, who was holding the door open.

" Everything all right? " he asked me in the foyer.

" Okay," I said.

" Thanks. I couldn't have handled it. Thanks a lot."

" It wasn't much."

" You handled it like an old pro," Harry said. " Psychology. You notice when you pick off the ringleader the rest of the mob backs down quick."

In the booth Amy Bell sat sipping her drink. I moved in across from her and sat down. She was silent for a moment. Then she looked up at me.

" It's a crazy world," she said, her voice a little sad. " Yesterday a senseless, vicious gunman murders a girl. To-night, in the very same town, a lady's honour is upheld. I say, Hurrah, hurrah, the age of chivalry is not entirely dead."

" Don't grind everything down," I said. " If it makes you feel any better it was a grudge fight. Ten years ago Joe Derechy stole my pogo stick. I've been tracking him down ever since."

" Laugh," she said. " That's the trouble with the world to-day. Nobody will admit to kindness because kindness is now considered weakness. So we laugh it off. Everything is a gag. Don't show your feelings.

What's the matter with us, anyway? And what's the matter with honest emotion, damn it? Is it out of style?"

"What with hot and cold wars, A-bombs and H-bombs, I guess the world is drained out of feelings. We're becoming robots, honey."

"Well, I confess right now you've given *me* a feeling," she said, touching her heart. "Right here where it counts. Stick around, dear."

"I had no intention of leaving," I said.

CHAPTER NINE

AMY BELL SANG several times that night. The patrons clamoured for encores and got them. I agreed with the customers. I could have listened to Amy Bell's throaty, vibrant voice for ever. It was so warm and intimate that you could have sworn she meant every word of love or loneliness in the lyrics.

While this was going on I sat in a corner booth in the dining-room. Amy would make frequent exits for costume changes and to freshen her make-up. About midnight, while she was away from the booth, Carl Podre showed up for the first time. He slid into the leather seat opposite me.

"What are you drinking?" he asked, signalling to a waiter.

"I've had my quota, Carl," I said. "One bourbon at the bar. Thanks."

"I've got some special venison steaks in the deep freeze," Podre said. "That and a salad——"

" No, thanks," I said. " Carl, I feel a little funny about all this. My wallet's been in my pocket all night and I've been taking up space."

" Don't be silly, kid," he said, smiling. " Harry told me how you handled those three drunks. Any time you want a job——"

" Not that kind," I said. " Tossing out drunks is not my idea of a future."

" Sure, you're right," he said. He turned to the waiter standing beside the booth and ordered a Scotch on the rocks for himself. " But I never figured you'd become a cop, either. You were always the studious type. What kind of course did you take at B.U. ? "

" Chemistry."

" So now you're a cop. It made your father happy, if nothing else."

" What's wrong with that? Does every kid have to make his old man miserable? "

" Hell, I admire you for it. Don't get me wrong, you're with a top outfit. Only I remember Paul telling me you never had the idea of becoming a trooper. Sure, I know what it means to your father. Him being in a wheel-chair and not getting anything out of life. The son comes along and carries on the family tradition. How many sons would do a thing like that? "

" You have it wrong, Carl," I said. " I like what I'm doing. There's the difference."

" Okay then." His drink came and he tasted it, savouring it. " And little Ellen Levesque, the cute kid next door? What happened there? I heard you two broke up."

" That was my fault, Carl," I said. " I kept getting

transferred. I had no right tying her down, waiting for me."

"Too bad," Podre said. "That's the way the dice roll sometimes." He looked at me closely, sensing, I suppose, that the subject wasn't agreeable to me. He said, "How was it in Korea, kid? Paul never wrote much. But maybe he wasn't to blame. I was on the move a lot then and hard to reach. But I'll tell you this. I wish it was me who got it instead of him."

You're such a glib liar, I thought. *In the first place you never worked hard in your life. You were always one of those angle boys. And in the second place, you skipped the draft in World War II by faking a nervous stomach and getting a crooked doctor to give you a false medical history. Two years later that doctor went to prison for illegal abortions. So don't try to kid me, Carl.*

"It's a damn shame about the Fedder girl," Podre was saying. "I liked her, Ralphie. One of those real good kids."

"I didn't know you knew her."

"I didn't, except off hand. Oh, I'd say hello to her if I'd see her in Sam Freeman's drugstore or in the grocery. The only time I really talked with her was when she came in here a month ago for a church donation. I paid off, Ralphie."

"Why not? You do business in this town, Carl."

"Sure, but I don't get ten bucks a week out of the townsfolks. The hundred I gave the Fedder girl was from the heart, Ralphie."

"Carl," I said. "Remember me? I happen to know you from 'way back, from your old poolroom days. So don't try to con me. These folks might not be your customers but they sure as hell control your licences and taxes."

He smiled. "Ralphie, I shouldn't have tried it on you. But it sounded good, didn't it?"

"Very touching," I said. "Did you ever sell phony gold-mining stock? You'd have been good at it."

"To me, that's a compliment," he said. "I was once in on a uranium deal. It didn't work out." He took a long draught from his drink. "How do you like Amy?" he asked suddenly.

"Great. I could listen to her forever. You're lucky to have her here, Carl."

"Yes, she draws the crowd. Lots of talent in her. She got off to a late start in this business but now she's going places. I don't want to hog the credit. But this is straight. She can thank me for it."

"She gives you the credit, Carl."

"She does, huh? Well, what do you know? This is a business where people use you and drop you." He seemed pleased, rolling the now empty glass in his fingers. "So she *does* give me the credit. Maybe it's because Amy and I were so friendly when she first came here. *Very* friendly, if you get what I mean."

"Oh," I said. I took out a cigarette and lit it. It didn't taste very good. "And how is it now?"

"Well, pretty good. Of course, she's a year older and a lot more sophisticated and I guess her stakes are higher. But things aren't bad."

"I wish you luck with her," I said.

I didn't fool him one bit because he chuckled and said, "What's the matter, Ralphie? You think you had the field all to yourself? With a girl like that you're bound to run into competition."

"I'm not even in the running," I said. "I was scratched at the start."

He waited for a moment before he spoke. "I'm not so sure of that," he said thoughtfully. Then he flashed me a brief smile, patted my shoulder and went off.

Amy finished at two in the morning. I was waiting for her in the foyer. There were some diners left in the main dining-room, and as she made her way through them, some spoke to her. She inclined her head and smiled graciously each time. At the edge of the foyer, she stopped to chat with Carl Podre. Podre turned, looked at me and shrugged his shoulders. Then Amy came over to me.

"Do you want to take me home?" she asked.

"That's why I was waiting," I said.

We went by the taproom where Harry was cleaning up. He said good night and we went outside The Red Wheel into the cool darkness. The big red-neon sign was off.

"I live only two blocks from here," Amy said, "and I don't have my car. Since I'm walking, and since we've had a murder, I need police protection."

I grinned. "If that's all you want, you can borrow my car."

"No, I want to walk the dark streets with you," she said. "It's a gorgeous night."

We went down the road, under the overhanging elms. There was a fragrant smell of flowers and freshly cut lawns. She began telling me about the place where she was staying. It belonged to a widow named Mrs. Danziger who rented out a few rooms.

" I stayed there last year, too," she said. " It's a charming, quaint old colonial. In my room I have an enormous four-poster bed that can sleep four people easily. And the food. Mrs. Danziger is just marvellous in the kitchen. I'm afraid I'll get fat before I finish my engagement here."

" When are you finishing? "

" In about ten days. I'm going to Salisbury Beach. Is that your territory, too? "

" Not this time of year. We have a summer sub-station there."

" There's no reason why you can't come to see me on your time off."

" Don't worry. I will."

Her high heels clicked along the pavement. " What was Carl saying to you to-night? "

" Nothing important."

" Anything about me? "

I hesitated a moment. " No," I lied.

We passed the corner of Montague Street. She peered down it but said nothing. Then we came to a large grey colonial house with a white portico. There was a light burning in front. A small, black wrought-iron sign said *Danziger*. In the driveway along the house I saw Amy's red convertible.

We turned in through a gate in a high, white slat fence. Up three steps to the portico. She rummaged in her handbag for her key, then said, " Thank you, Ralph, and good night."

" Wait a minute," I said. I was facing her. Now my arms went around her, circling her waist, pulling her in. I bent my head, my mouth seeking hers. She averted her face with smooth expertness and laughed.

" You have the impetuousness of youth, dear," she said. " Don't hurry things so much."

" It's a short life," I said. " A lot shorter than you think."

" Poof. For you? At *your* age? What's the matter? Your job scare you? "

" No. Not my job."

" Disillusionment," she said. " You had a disappointing love affair and now you're on the rebound. Is that the score? "

" That's a fast shot in the dark," I said.

" My womanly intuition. You seem to think you have to make up for lost time. Who was she, dear? "

" The usual girl next door."

" You were going to be married? "

" We set the date twice. Each time something happened. Now she's afraid we're jinxed. She won't set another date, that's for sure."

" You could elope."

" I asked her. She doesn't consider it proper. She's a very proper girl."

" Good for her," Amy said. " Marriage is the biggest thing in a girl's life. All of us want the orange blossoms and the white gown and the church. I wouldn't settle for less, either."

" I'm glad you're the sentimental type," I said, drawing her in again.

She kept her face averted, but rubbed my cheek with her scented fingers. " Don't rush it, dear. I like you a lot, I really do. But I have to be led up to it in stages. I don't like to be pawed on a front porch."

" I'm sorry," I said.

She smiled and pulled my head down. Her soft

mouth covered mine, clung a moment, then let go. " There," she said softly. " That's just for walking me home."

" When do I see you again? "

" You tell *me*, dear."

" I don't go back on duty until five in the afternoon. Will you take a ride with me before then? "

" You have yourself a date," she said. " Phone me here." Her key went into the lock. " Good night, dear."

I watched her go inside. The door closed. I stood there feeling a sense of buoyancy in me. Then I floated down the stairs as though I weighed only five pounds. The walk back to my car took only three minutes. I got into the Ford, started it and drove back to Cambridge.

CHAPTER TEN

I CALLED HER from Cambridge about eleven in the morning. Mrs. Danziger told me she was still asleep. I called her again at one and this time I spoke to her. She told me she would be tied up until three. I said I would drop around at that time.

I came back to Dorset, passing The Red Wheel. A shiny beach wagon was parked at the side door with the words THE RED WHEEL inscribed in bright red letters on the door panel. Harry, the bartender, was unloading supplies from the back of it. I tooted my horn and he looked around, smiled broadly and waved at me.

Promptly on the hour of three I was at the Danziger house. It was a warm, gentle day with a slight, cooling sea breeze blowing in from the Atlantic.

When she had spoken to me on the phone, she had seemed very gay and zestful. Now as she came down the stairs her face was solemn and thoughtful. She said quietly, " Let's use my car, dear. It's such a beautiful day and we can ride with the top down."

We went into the driveway and put down the top of her convertible. I drove, heading the car out towards Pond Road.

" Where are you going? " she asked.

" I know a spot," I said. " It's quiet and peaceful and there's a good view."

" Do you have an especially well conceived plan of operation to-day? "

" About what? "

" I'm beginning to question your motives, young man." She took a cigarette from her bag and used the dash lighter to fire it. " You're taking me riding. I was thinking why should you? I'm older than you are."

" What has age got to do with it? I happen to like you, Amy. And why this sudden seriousness? "

" I've been giving it a lot of thought," she said. " I don't want to get sucked into a whirlpool." She drew deeply on her cigarette. " Every man has little wheels turning in his mind," she continued bitterly. " He wants something. And I'm beginning to get an idea what you want, Daddy-o. A quiet spot where we can be away from prying eyes."

" That's a rough way of saying it, Amy."

" Under this smooth Pan-cake make-up I'm a rough girl."

" I don't think you are, Amy."

" Next comes the profound observation that my defence mechanism is working."

" I had an idea like that, yes."

" So you're all set for an afternoon of hot romance. Is that it? "

" Dammit," I said. " All right. Yes. And if you knew it why did you come along? "

" Because I get a kick out of you," she said soberly. " You're an eager kid. And, I think, a good kid. Direct and honest, with no fakery. It's been a refreshing experience."

" Sure. I can see you're all thrilled about it."

She reached out and patted my hand on the steering wheel. " I'm sorry. I'm not at my best to-day and I'm taking it out on you. The truth is I'm a very lonely person. I like company, honestly. And I'd rather be with you than with any man I've met in my life. The ones I know consist of middle-aged, married wolves, with panting breaths and fumbling hands. They make me feel like a second-rate call girl. I don't feel that way with you, dear."

" Thanks," I said. " It's a small consolation."

" You don't understand," she said carefully. " I have to watch myself. I can't afford to go overboard for a young trooper in a crew haircut. I've a long rocky road ahead of me and I'm not getting tangled up in any sweet, sticky, gooey love. If you want to have a little company and a few laughs, fine. Otherwise, turn around and we'll go back."

I didn't know what was bothering her, but I didn't

turn around. I kept driving. We passed the Derechy cottage and made the turn along the pond. After we came over the rise in the hill, I slowed the car, swung it around and parked it at the edge of the bluff.

" This is the spot," I said. " Ever been here? "

" No," she said. " And frankly, I don't see anything special about the view."

" I didn't promise any Grand Canyon."

" How many girls have you had here before? "

" You're making me sound like a big operator. I've had nobody here before. Yesterday was the first time I saw this place. You're the first, Amy."

" I'm honoured," she said, her body relaxing in the seat. " What do you feel like doing? "

I grinned. " I'm surprised you'd lead with such a loaded question."

" Besides *that*," she said, two tiny colour spots appearing in her cheeks. " What's the next best thing you'd like to do? "

" I've got a crazy idea I'd like to walk down to the pond, take off my shoes and stockings and wade in the water."

" That's your youth speaking again. I'll walk down with you, but I won't join in the hilarious, mad festivities."

There was a steep narrow path that led down to the water. I helped Amy out of the car and we followed the path. She looked quickly at the nearest cottage two hundred yards away, half-hidden by the trees. It was the one where the windows were covered by boiler plating.

" Your reputation is safe," I said, watching her.

"All these cottages are shuttered and nobody's around. Terrific spot, isn't it?"

" Rave on," she said. " I've been taken in by a sales talk." She was walking behind me now. I was pushing bushes from her path so the brambles wouldn't catch on her wind-billowing skirt. Near the shore the dual dirt tracks wound down from the bluff and continued into the woods. At the edge of the tracks I saw a small black object on the ground. I bent down and picked it up. It was a woman's brooch shaped like a spider web.

" Hey," I said, turning. " Treasure."

" It's mine," she said instantly. Then her hand came up and covered her mouth.

" Yours? " I asked.

She laughed shortly. " That's the greed in me. I mean we found it together. You wouldn't have any use for it."

" Sure," I said, holding it out. " Take it."

She made no move towards it. " I've changed my mind. It's old and dirty and worthless. Why would I want the ugly thing? "

I rubbed it with my fingers. The blacking started to come off. " It's sterling silver and it's been laying around for a few months. We have some stuff at the barracks. I bet if I polish it for you——"

" I said I don't want it," she said, her breath hissing out between her teeth. " Furthermore, I have a headache. Let's go back."

We climbed up the hill to the car. " I want to go home," she said. " I'll drive."

" Suppose you tell me what's wrong," I said, opening the car door for her.

" Nothing's wrong. I have a splitting headache. And sometimes I get very fed up with rustic beauty. This is one of those days I long for the tall, cool spires of skyscrapers."

I got in beside her. " The headache," I said, " is the most convenient excuse yet devised by modern woman."

She didn't answer. She turned the car around and started it down the hill. I began rubbing the brooch with my handkerchief, at the same time straightening out the bent strands of the cobweb. On the back of the brooch, just below the clasp, I saw the initials *A.B.*

I turned and stared at her. " So it *is* really yours."

" What is? "

" The brooch. It has your initials on the back. A.B."

" Now isn't that a coincidence."

" Is it? "

" Let's not get silly about it," she said. " It's not mine. I never saw it before in my life. A.B. can be Annette Banks or Amantha Bilgewater or Aggie Blimp or a thousand other names. Don't belabour the point."

" I wouldn't. Only you're a bit touchy about it."

" Because I don't like the way you play detective with me. I never particularly cared for cops anyway."

" If that's the case——" I started to say stiffly.

" I know," she said wearily. " Why did I go out with you. Because you're not an ordinary cop. And also because I didn't expect you to play policeman twenty-four hours a day." Then, impulsively, she reached out and squeezed my hand. " I'm sorry. Really I am. I've been a little jumpy to-day and I'm taking it out on you. Forgive me, dear."

" It's all right," I said. " I hope I——"

" Of course. It's one of my off days. Come see me again on your next free time. I promise I'll be sweeter."

She let me off at Mrs. Danziger's. We made no specific date. She made no effort to kiss me good-bye this time, nor, from her hurried attitude, did I expect it. I said I would phone her then drove off in my Ford.

She hadn't deceived me about the silver cobweb pin, though. It was hers. And although it was my first time on the bluff with another person, it wasn't her first time. Whatever had happened there brought back no pleasurable memories to her. The condition of the brooch could have meant it had lain there since last summer. And last summer was the time Carl Podre had mentioned about being so *very* friendly with her.

CHAPTER ELEVEN

I RETURNED to the barracks at four. I parked my car in the rear lot and went up the garage stairs to the guardroom. Trooper Tony Pellegrini was at the desk in the duty office when I checked in there.

Upstairs in my room, Keith Ludwell was in uniform. He sat near the bureau putting a polish on his black leather holster.

" How's the Fedder case going? " I asked, starting to strip down.

" Not bad," he said. " There's a new development.

A Boston detective saw Whitey Swenke at a ball game five weeks ago. That was two weeks before the Newburyport bank job. Swenke was with George Hozak."

" Why didn't the cop grab them? "

" He didn't recognise Swenke at the time."

" He could have picked up Hozak."

" For what? Hozak was out on bail at the time for another robbery. Anyway, now the brass think there's a tie-in between Swenke and Hozak on the Newburyport bank job. There's a fourteen-state G.A. out on Hozak. They think Hozak could have been the one who was wounded by the cop and he may be hiding out in the Ipswich area. If he is, that gives Swenke a good reason for hiring the truck. He was going to transport Hozak in it."

" I don't know if that's such big news," I said. " They were working along those lines anyway."

" But this is stronger confirmation of it," Ludwell said.

" What are they getting out of Swenke? "

" A lot of injured innocence."

I went to the closet for my blue breeches. I was knotting my black silk tie in front of the mirror when Ludwell finished polishing his holster.

He said, " Have you seen the captain yet? "

" No," I said, turning around. " Did he want to see me? "

" Yes," Ludwell said. " He's waiting to talk to you. I thought you saw him on the way in. He was in the dining-room."

I fastened the silver clip with the state shield on it. " You have any idea what it's about? "

"No. Must be the Fedder case. You haven't done anything wrong, have you?"

"I don't think so," I said. "But in this job you never know."

He was waiting for me in the dining-room. When I walked in Captain Dondera handed me a letter and said, simply, "Read this, Lindsey."

I looked at the envelope. It was postmarked Dorset and addressed to *Commanding Officer, Topsfield Barracks, State Police, Topsfield, Mass.*

I opened the flap and took out a single sheet of cheap notepaper. There was no date. The letter was typed. It read:

Dear Sir:

I must report some disgraceful conduct on the part of one of your troopers. The other night at midnight I observed this trooper leaving a State Police blue cruiser and entering The Red Wheel in Dorset. When he came out he was leading a drunken teen-age boy to a Cadillac sedan. The boy was so badly under the influence of liquor that he had to be put into the back seat of the car. I think it's a terrible thing when one of your men, who has probably received a bribe, will cover up the fact that the Red Wheel is serving liquor to minors. I am sure you will take quick and drastic action.

Patriotic Observer.

I refolded the notepaper, put it carefully back into the envelope and handed it back to Captain Dondera.

" Sit down, Lindsey," he said.

I sat down, facing him across the table.

Dondera said, " It's a lousy letter for us to get."

" Yes, sir," I said. " But it's not the whole truth, Captain. I wish I knew who's accusing me of——"

" We've checked with Corporal Kerrigan," Dondera interrupted. " We know the real story. But that doesn't mean you used sound judgment that night. If I'd been the trooper I would have brought this boy in and tossed him in a cell."

" That was explained to me."

" I'm glad it was. On your own responsibility you made the decision. It's done with, Lindsey. But you'll have to make similar decisions time and time again. When to make a pinch and when not to make a pinch. I don't like to see a man arrest-happy. But on the other hand, I don't want him to be timid, either."

" Yes, sir."

" An anonymous letter like this harms the prestige we've built up through the years. We don't like to get them. Yet, these kind of tips are very important to us. Without informants the police would get nowhere. Lots of times it's the only way we have of knowing of any wrongdoing."

" I understand, Captain."

" Some information is worthless, malicious, or deliberate grudge stuff. What this one is I don't know. It's either an honest mistake on somebody's part, or somebody is out to get you. Do *you* know? "

" No, sir."

" You've been here about a week. Have you had trouble with anybody? "

" No, sir."

" How about traffic violations? "

" I booked eight or nine. Ludwell did the rest."

" You have any trouble with any of them? "

" No, Captain."

" How about Swenke? Didn't he threaten you or something? "

" No, Captain. He said he'd remember my name. I don't know if it was a threat or not. It might have been only conversation."

" And it might not," Dondera said. " Of course, Swenke himself couldn't have written the letter. He's in jail and his mail is censored. Also, it's too well written. But I'm wondering if he has a friend or two in Dorset. That's what bothers me. I'd hate to think that any of his pals are running around loose in this area." He put the letter into his pocket. " That'll be all, Lindsey. I'll have the case sergeant look into it before we decide what action to take with you. Meanwhile you'll write a full report on it. And I wouldn't mention it to anybody. Not even our own boys."

" Yes, sir," I said.

I went out on patrol that evening with Keith Ludwell. As we drove down U.S. 1 in Cruiser 29, he asked, " Everything all right? "

" Fine," I said, although I knew it wasn't fine. I had made a mistake in judgment. I would be disciplined for it and it would go on my record.

" You been seeing Miss Bell? " he asked.

" Yes," I said, turning to him curiously. " How did you know, Keith? "

" Dorset's a small town, Ralph. It's like living in a goldfish bowl."

" I'm beginning to realise that."

It had started to rain and I didn't like it. Rain meant slippery roads, and wet, slippery roads meant accidents. Blobs of big raindrops were hitting the windshield and Ludwell set the windshield wipers moving. Not looking at me, but watching the road, he said, " I never thought you'd end up by making a date with the girl."

I grinned. " I've got a habit of working fast."

He frowned. He was always frowning and pulling his eyebrows down. I don't remember ever seeing him smile. He said, " Well, that's your business, Ralph. But I myself wouldn't get mixed up with that kind of stuff."

" Why not? I don't see anything wrong with it. She's a nice girl. And why is it that I've been picked up on every single thing I do? "

" Who's picking on you? Not me."

" I've been in Topsfield a week and I've been constantly wrong. In everything. Even the Westlake kid is sore at me for not killing Swenke. And what anybody misses, you pick up, Keith."

" I'm senior man to you, Ralph. It's my job and responsibility to finish training you and set you off on the right road. It's for your own good, isn't it? "

" Yes, I guess so," I said, thinking it was no use, you couldn't penetrate Ludwell's hard shell. " I'm sorry I blew my stack, Keith."

" It's okay, I know how it is. For a kid who's been in the troops only four months you came here with a big reputation. Sometimes that's no good. It gives a man a big head. You have a lot to learn yet. I'd say you've been damn lucky. You have an in with the brass. Your father is an ex-trooper and left quite a name with the outfit. Naturally, when a good assignment came up, they gave you a break."

That was one thing that was always hinted to me. My father's influence with G.H.Q. and Detective-Lieutenant Newpole. The truth was I had only worked on two special assignments and it was only the first one that had anything to do with my father.

"You see what I mean, don't you?" Ludwell was saying. "You came here with a big jump over the others. The rest of us have to do it the hard way. I've got almost three enlistments in and I haven't made stripes yet."

"You're on only six years," I said. "You're young yet."

"I'm twenty-eight."

"You're due pretty soon. And don't think I've got such a big jump. I've been in the doghouse as much as anybody."

"One thing about me," Ludwell said, "I've never been in the doghouse. I've worked hard and stuck to the job. There's no reason why I shouldn't make corporal this year. My monthly activity report is good. I'm senior trooper here. Before you came I was getting more desk work than any of the others. Then they put you on with me. That gave me more patrol work."

"I'm sorry if I'm the cause of any——"

"Oh, no," he said quickly. "I don't mind at all. If I can make a good trooper out of you it'll show on my record at G.H.Q. I weigh everything I do. That's why, some day, I'm going to be captain and command this troop."

"I think you will at that," I said.

" If I watch myself and don't make any mistakes."

" You're not the type who makes mistakes, Keith."

" The main idea is not to worry about money. Money worries affect your work. That's why marriage would be a mistake now. Rank means money, so you don't saddle yourself with a wife and kids until you have some rank. Simple? And that's why a trooper has to make the right marriage. The type of wife is important, too. Some girl with a good family and important political background."

The windshield wipers were clicking like a metronome. I said, " You mean a wife with political influence."

" That's the general idea. A wife with connections does no harm."

" So that wouldn't include any waitresses," I said.

His eyebrows came down and that frown showed on his face. " You mean the girl at the Dorset Diner. Her name's Marsha Gordioni and I don't see her for dust."

" She doesn't think so, Keith. I've seen the look in her eyes."

" Well, that's *her* business."

" Do you think it's fair? "

He looked at me, surprised. " What do you mean? "

" I don't see you discouraging it."

" Listen, Ralph, on this job you have to pay attention to small details. A cop is as good as the information he's able to get. Marsha gives me a lot of tips in this area. I have others in different sections. That's why I'm nice to *everybody*. It pays off. One thing to remember is this. The uniform you're wearing pulls a lot of weight. You can get a lot of stuff other cops

can't get. That's because people have respect and confidence in you."

" I don't know," I said. " I haven't been getting much of either."

" It's because you look kind of young. That's a little handicap. But here's what I want to bring out. Don't get yourself mixed up with the wrong kind of dames. I've seen troopers get the heave-ho on account of it."

I think he would have continued to lecture me, but just then we got a Signal 16 that there was a bad car accident on U.S. 1 in Newburyport.

CHAPTER TWELVE

BECAUSE OF the distance we arrived at the scene after a cruiser from our Salisbury Beach sub-station was already there. The accident car, a glossy new Plymouth, had gone off the road and wrapped itself around a tree. The two Salisbury troopers were putting a man in a sailor uniform into a stretcher, getting ready to transport him to the Anna Jaques Hospital in Newburyport.

" You handle the witnesses," Ludwell said to me. " It's good experience for you."

I put on my pale blue raincoat while Ludwell went up the road, set a flare in the ground and got the traffic unsnarled. We had frequent accidents of this type. Servicemen who had short leaves would try to make Philadelphia or Washington or Ohio, spend

D

two days there and return, all in three days. Many times they were so tired from the hypnosis of constant high-speed driving that they would fall asleep at the wheel.

The Salisbury cruiser, siren growling, sped away from the scene. In it was the stretcher installed lengthwise across the back and front seats, with one of the troopers sitting in back at the victim's head.

I went to work, talking to witnesses, writing pages in my book, resigned to the fact that I would have many hours of reports later. I was just about finished when I saw a newspaper car stop up the road where Ludwell stood, wearing his white cross straps and holding his flashlight. He walked toward the wreck with a news photographer, explaining the accident to him in his sincere, polite, public-relations manner. Then, as the photographer began flashing pictures, he took two of Ludwell, who stood there, his face serious and stern, the rain slanting against him and glistening on the silver buttons of his raincoat.

After the tow truck came for the wreck, we cleared the area and went back on patrol. We would contact the Salisbury troopers later to complete the investigation.

" Don't ride me about the pictures," Ludwell said. " You know how those news photographers are. They grab the first cop they see and take his picture. It doesn't mean a thing."

That was what he said to me. I don't think he meant anything of the kind. I had an idea that pictures, any news pictures, were important to Ludwell. They would be seen by the brass at G.H.Q. and remembered. When the promotion list came up with Ludwell on it, the brass would be more familiar with him. Publicity would never do Ludwell any harm.

At midnight we drove into Dorset and parked in front of the diner. The sky was heavy with clouds but the storm had passed. I saw the polishing cloth come out of Ludwell's pocket. He wiped his boots and belts, brushed his uniform carefully, set his cap exactly right and went inside.

The waitress, Marsha Gordioni, ran over to him as he made for his booth. There was a lot of animated conversation after she brought him his food. The counterman came over and talked, too. One truck driver, a toothpick sticking from the corner of his mouth, joined the group, leaning into the booth and offering an occasional comment.

I sat in the cruiser, looking over at The Red Wheel and wondering what Amy Bell was doing. Fifteen minutes later, Ludwell came out of the diner and it was my turn to go in.

I stood just inside the door, sniffing the aroma of fresh coffee. The waitress came up, smiled and pointed to the booth Ludwell had vacated. I studied her as she set down a glass of water and handed me a plastic-covered menu. She was a tall, well-rounded girl with coiled hair too blonde to be natural. She had a curved, red, wet mouth and damp, doglike brown eyes. She said, " You're the new trooper Keith is training. Ralph Lindsey? "

" That's me." I smiled up at her. " I'm what they call a boot."

" What do you think of Keith? " she asked. " Don't you think he's just wonderful? "

" I sure do," I said. " I'll have a ham sandwich on rye, coffee and apple pie."

She wrote the order impatiently on a slip. " You're lucky to have Keith training you. I think he's the most terrific trooper I've ever seen."

She went away. I smoked a cigarette and waited. When she came back with my order, she sat down opposite me. Her eyebrows arched as I began to eat. I started to feel uncomfortable. Anyone does when somebody stares at them while they are eating.

" What's wrong? " I asked. " Am I using the wrong fork? "

" Oh, no," she said. " I was thinking you're awfully young."

" I'm twenty-three."

" Are you? You don't look twenty-three. I wouldn't take you for more than nineteen or twenty."

" I've been voting for two years. Doesn't that make me an adult citizen? "

" I don't think you're going to be all grown up until Keith finishes with you. He'll teach you a lot. Keith has broken a lot of cases around here. It surprises me he isn't a sergeant, or even a lieutenant. Do you think politics or jealousy has anything to do with it? "

" It all takes time," I said. " He's young yet. But don't worry, he'll get there."

" Oh, I know that," she said. " How do you like the Topsfield Barracks? "

" Fine."

" You just do everything Keith tells you and you won't go wrong." She examined her silver-lacquered fingernails. Then, " Does Keith ever say anything about me? "

"Oh, yes," I said, my mouth full of the sandwich. "He's spoken of you."

"He has? What did he say?"

"All nice things," I said, chewing and swallowing.

"Exactly what?"

I swallowed again. "I don't recall the exact words, but they were all nice things."

She looked around, then lowered her voice. "I go out with Keith. Keep it confidential because he doesn't like it to be known around here. He said it wouldn't look right because he eats here and people would think he gets a handout. But he doesn't. He pays for every single thing. Out of his own pocket."

I nodded and took another bite out of the sandwich. Her last sentence wasn't exactly true. Keith didn't pay for the food out of his own pocket. Every trooper got a dollar from the barracks for his midnight snack.

"I've been married," she said, "and I have a little daughter. My husband and I were divorced and I live with my mother in Rowley. Keith and I, when we go out, go to some quiet place and have a few beers. I don't go out with any other men." Her hands were moving nervously on the table and I was beginning to feel sorry for her. She said, almost wistfully, "Do you know if Keith goes out with other girls?"

I couldn't talk at the moment because I was chewing another mouthful of food. But she didn't wait for an answer. A laugh came out of her, a little, unsure laugh. She said, "I don't want Keith to think I'm pressing him. You know what I mean. A man doesn't like to be pressed."

"Sure," I said, swallowing. "I don't know if he

sees any other girls. He never discussed his private life with me, Marsha."

Her mouth made an O. "How did you know my name?"

"Keith told me."

Her eyes glistened. "If he told you my name, I think it means something, don't you? Otherwise he wouldn't mention my name to you."

I sipped my coffee and cut into the apple pie, hurrying it so that I could get away from the cloying atmosphere as quickly as I could. I was becoming a little bitter at Ludwell.

"Keith is working on that terrible Mary Fedder murder." she said, her voice a little hushed. " I've been able to help him a little. I told him plenty about the strange men who are around here during the racing season. They'd just as soon make a pass at a girl as light a cigarette. They're always making passes at me. This Swenke might have tried to get fresh with Mary Ann. She could have spurned him and he got revenge."

She had been reading too many confession magazines. I said, " Mary Fedder had been going to college in Boston the last four years. When she did come home to Dorset, she never went anywhere without Russell Westlake. And he never took her any place where a person like Swenke might hang around. I'll bet Mary and Westlake never came in here."

"That's not so," she said. "Russell Westlake and she came in here quite a few times on the way home from a movie."

"But you never saw Whitey Swenke here."

"No. But he might have come in when I was off."

" Nobody here remembers Swenke. And Westlake never saw him before."

" Keith will find out the truth," she said. " He's so quick and clever about everything. Nobody can put anything past him."

" Sure," I said. In her rosy-clouded mind she had the idea that Trooper Keith Ludwell was in charge of the case and was going to solve it singlehandedly.

" I don't want to take anything away from you," she said. " But, of course, you got a big break when you captured Whitey Swenke. It could have been the other way around, you know."

" You mean Swenke could have captured me? "

" No, no," she said. " I mean Keith got the first call. When he came to the Fedder house he had to stay there and see if the girl needed medical attention. He couldn't chase the murderer."

" No," I said. " He couldn't."

" So you got the second call. You happened to be in the right spot to capture Swenke. Keith should have been given *some* of the credit. I think the newspapers were very unfair. It was plain luck. If you had had Keith's patrol and he had had yours it would have been the other way around."

By now her voice had grown hostile as though I were to blame that our positions hadn't been reversed. I said, " Yes, life is funny that way. A flip of the coin."

" Sometimes people just don't get the breaks."

" I'm not so sure," I said. " Keith is working on the case and I'm not."

" Oh," she said, brightening. " You're not? "

" No. So you can see which one of us is more important to the skipper."

That made her a lot happier. When I paid my check and said good-bye to her she actually beamed at me.

In the cruiser, Ludwell said, " What was Marsha bending your ear about? "

" All about you."

He frowned a little. " Is there anything wrong with that? "

" You're old enough to know what you're doing," I said. " I'm in no position to advise the senior man."

" No, you're not."

" I'll tell you this," I said. " I'm ambitious, too, Keith. Not only for myself. I've got a father who thinks a lot of this business. I'm not just putting my time in towards a pension. You might find me up there competing with you for that troop captaincy some day."

" I don't think so," he said. " I've got a six-year jump on you and my record is spotless. Let's see if yours will be like that in six years."

" Maybe it won't be spotless," I said. " But if I ever do make it up there, it'll be on my own. I don't believe I'd take advantage of a woman in order to make it."

" You're young," he said, his voice calm and un-ruffled. " You've got a lot to learn, boy."

" Yes," I said. " I'm learning all the time. Especially about people. Let's ride, Keith."

We arrived back at the barracks at three in the morning. Ludwell took his shower, came back to the room, clipped his fingernails, fussed with the wrinkles in his sheet until he had the bed perfectly smooth, then turned in. Shortly afterwards he was asleep, breathing slowly and evenly.

I lay back on the bed staring up in the darkness, thinking of Amy Bell and the silver cobweb brooch. She had lost it, apparently a year ago. There must have been some important reason why she had denied ownership so vehemently. When I had the chance I would look in the files and see what had happened in the area last summer.

I had been asleep less than three hours when I awoke. The light was on in the room and Ludwell was nudging me. He was already in uniform and was buckling on his leather equipment. From the other rooms I could hear troopers moving about. Bleary-eyed I sat up and looked out of the window. It was still dark outside. I asked Ludwell what the emergency was.

He was checking his revolver. Now he looked at me with bright, hard eyes.

He said, " Russell Westlake has disappeared."

CHAPTER THIRTEEN

TROOPERS WERE milling around in the kitchen, some of them still half-dressed like myself, strapping puttees, knotting ties, gulping steaming coffee. While we were at it, Corporal Kerrigan was explaining to us that Westlake had been last seen yesterday afternoon. He had left home without saying where he was going. At midnight he had not returned. His worried family began calling relatives and friends as far away as New

York. Nobody had seen or heard from him. At five-thirty in the morning they had finally called Chief Rigsby. A few minutes later we had been awakened.

"We don't know what this is yet," Kerrigan said. "The kid was upset. Maybe he took off and is halfway to Chicago. Maybe he's on a binge and shacked up with a blonde in a Boston hotel. Or maybe he's cracked up his car and is hurt. Or maybe he's done the Dutch act and he's got a tube running from the exhaust of his car inside. I've sent out a File 6 on the teletype, but we've all got a job to do. Each of you is going to be given a description of Westlake and his car."

Then he gave out the assignments. Wisnioski on U.S. 1 to the Peabody-Danvers line, checking every motor court and bylane for Westlake or his car. At the Peabody line the Andover Barracks would carry on. Doherty north to the Newburyport line, doing the same thing, meeting the patrols from the Salisbury sub-station. Swanson west on a jagged sweep from George-town to Middleton. Ludwell on the Route 1 express-way as far as the New Hampshire state line. Pellegrini directly east as far as Gloucester. All cities and towns with established police departments and communications would conduct their own search.

"Ralph," he said to me, "you stick around. I might need a man for something else."

The others tramped out of the kitchen, through the dining-room and guardroom, and clattered down the stairs to the garage. The cruisers started up and roared away.

I went with Kerrigan into the duty office. Chief Rigsby, in leather jacket and duck-billed cap was sitting on the bench talking to a man with a deeply-lined face and iron-grey hair. I was introduced to him. He was Ernest Westlake, father of Russell Westlake.

The detectives and the brass would arrive soon. Meanwhile Kerrigan was trying to take the father out of the shock and inertia that were gripping him. Kerrigan said, " We'll all have a cup of good hot coffee. You'd be surprised how the coffee will perk you up, Mr. Westlake."

Ernest Westlake shook his head in mute refusal.

" Don't you worry, Mr. Westlake," Chief Rigsby said. " If Russell's car is anywhere around in the state it'll be found. There's a regular system for those things."

Mr. Westlake stared straight ahead and said tonelessly, " My boy was in a bad turmoil."

Kerrigan moved in behind his desk and sat down. He took out a pad of paper and began writing. " We know your boy was upset, Mr. Westlake. It's only natural. Does he ever take a drink? "

Westlake swallowed, looked down and said, " My boy doesn't drink, Corporal."

" There's always a first time, sir. I wouldn't blame him any in an emotional disturbance like this."

" My boy doesn't drink," Mr. Westlake said.

" Do you know of any place he might go? Somebody he might want to talk to, to get it off his chest? "

" We've called everybody, Corporal."

" Has he been taking any kind of medication, sir? "

" No."

" Has he indicated he might do something desperate? "

" That's what's been bothering me," Mr. Westlake

said, his eyes wandering around the room. "The way he's been acting, I'm afraid for him."

"Why are you afraid, Mr. Westlake? Has he been despondent?"

"No, not what you'd call despondent. I'd say he was—grim. Russell was determined to get to the bottom of things. He wasn't satisfied with the police investigation. He said they were too slow, too methodical. He had some ideas of his own. He was going to find out."

"He was going to find out what, sir?" Kerrigan asked.

"I don't know. He said he could do better than you."

"A lot of people feel that way," Kerrigan said. "And once in a while they accomplish something where we don't. Usually, it's because they have some information we don't have. Trouble is, sir, sometimes they'll go about it illegally."

"My boy would never do anything illegal, Corporal."

"Sure, he wouldn't," Kerrigan said. "But I'm wondering just what information Russell has withheld from us. That's the biggest trouble we have, Mr. Westlake."

Mr. Westlake took a deep breath. "Russell did say he had an idea about something. What it was I don't know."

I moved in closer. "Mr. Westlake," I said. I saw Kerrigan staring at me for interfering, but I went on. "Mr. Westlake, what about your son's honeymoon?"

Westlake turned to me. "What about it?"

" Had he planned a honeymoon, sir? "

" Yes, the children were going to have a honeymoon. A week."

" Where were they going, sir? " I asked. " I mean, did they have reservations anywhere? Tickets of some kind? "

Westlake shook his head. " No. You see, Russell and Mary Ann were pretty sensible. They didn't plan on any lavish honeymoon. They wanted to buy a little house some day. None of us knew where they were going. But I assure you it would be no place expensive."

" Even if it wasn't, sir, you'd think they'd mention their hotel or resort reservation."

" No. It was all a big secret. And some kind of funny secret, too. Because everytime any of the family brought up the subject of the honeymoon the two children would laugh as though it were a big joke."

" Then possibly," I said, " they weren't going to have a honeymoon at all. Maybe they decided not to live with the Fedders but to go right into housekeeping. If we could find the house they rented, maybe Russell went there and is staying——"

" No," Westlake said. " They were definitely going on a week's honeymoon because Russell had notified them at the mill. As for housekeeping, they planned to live with the Fedders two years to save money to buy a house of their own."

" But can you be absolutely sure, sir? "

" We're sure. They were packing wedding gifts and storing them in the attic. Silverware, linens, utensils. If they were going to rent a house they wouldn't have done that, would they? "

" No, sir," I said. " I guess not."

I sat down on the bench and smoked a cigarette. I wasn't doing any better than Kerrigan or Rigsby.

By seven o'clock Sergeant Neal had arrived, cutting short his day off. Then Captain Crow, the adjutant, came down from G.H.Q. with Detective-Lieutenant Ed Newpole. Captain Dondera, the troop commander, arrived shortly afterwards. There were a great many teletype, telephone and radio messages.

I received no assignment. At eight o'clock I was ordered into fatigues and sent down to the garage to wash motor-cycles. At eight-forty-five I heard heavy footsteps jogging down the stairs to the cars in the parking area. Detectives got into their black cruisers and sped away. Lieutenant Newpole came down, half-running for his car. He saw me standing there in wet-stained fatigues and holding a dripping water hose.

" Keeping you busy? " he asked.

" Yes, sir," I said. " What's all the commotion, Lieutenant? "

" Russell Westlake," Newpole said.

" They found him? "

" His car. Pellegrini found it abandoned in Ipswich. It was on Line Brook Road along the edge of the state forest."

" And Westlake himself? "

" No sign of him yet," Newpole said. He waited for Captain Crow to join him, then got into the cruiser, spun it around and raced out of the parking lot.

I went back to washing motor-cycles. A few minutes

later Corporal Kerrigan called down to me to come up and get back into uniform. He said I might be needed somewhere.

By noon they had established one significant fact. The abandoned car had been examined by the technical experts, who found all fingerprints had been wiped from it.

At 1.15 p.m. the bloodhounds, which had been sent down from the Andover Barracks, were returned to their kennels. They had been unable to pick up any scent of Westlake in the area. By this time a posse had been formed by troopers from Andover, Concord, Salisbury and Topsfield. Joining them in a search of the Willowdale State Forest were the local police and civilian volunteers. At the Salem County Jail Whitey Swenke was grilled about his associates. No information. The general alarm for George Hozak was repeated. No sign of Russell Westlake.

Through all this I was fretting impatiently at the barracks. Finally, at two o'clock, I was ordered to take out a blue cruiser and work with Chief Rigsby.

He was waiting for me downstairs in the rear parking lot. His car was an old 1948 Pontiac, the paint a faded, chalky blue, but with a motor that hummed like a contented cat.

He said, " They suggest we use two cars. Yours has a shortwave radio, mine doesn't. Also, we might have to separate to save time."

" Where are we going? " I asked.

He fiddled with his duck-billed cap. " Just because they found Russell Westlake's car in Ipswich, that doesn't mean the kid was there."

" No. Not when somebody took the trouble to wipe off all prints."

He nodded. " There are a few hangouts around Dorset where the kids park and look at the moon. I figure we ought to check every one of them. Russell might have been nosing around one of those places and something happened to him."

" I know one good spot. The bluff at Dorset Pond."

" I've already been there. I tried that first. There are others. I know them all." He wiped his hands on his work pants. " I hope you don't think it's a waste of time working with me."

" No," I said. " Why do you say that, Chief? "

" Nothing," he said. He brushed a bead of sweat from his brow, as though anxious to do something with his hands. " Dorset's a small town and there aren't too many places to look. I didn't think they'd waste the time of a trooper going with me."

" One thing they taught me." I said. " Nothing's ever wasted."

" Anyway, I don't think we'll find Russell." His voice was bleak and far away. " I've got a feeling Russell is dead."

CHAPTER FOURTEEN

WE DIDN'T FIND Russell Westlake that Friday afternoon. We worked until five, covering every spot where young people were apt to go. We asked many questions of many people. The work was thorough, but nothing came of it.

Returning to the barracks I had to thread my way through crowds of newspapermen and photographers. In the guardroom I saw the captain of detectives had come down from G.H.Q. and was surrounded by his plain-clothes men. Nobody else had found Russell Westlake, either.

I was getting ready to wash up for supper when I got a call to report to the duty office. As soon as I came in Sergeant Neal told me to sit down and wait. He walked out of the room. Then Captain Dondera, the troop commander, came in and sat down behind the desk.

" Ralph," he said, " the postman seems to like us. We got another letter. How'd you like to look at this one? "

He took an envelope out of the desk drawer and passed it over to me. My heart gave a skip as I looked at the address. It was the same as the first one. A Dorset postmark. Inside was the same notepaper, the typing on it said:

Dear Sir:

I think it's disgusting that a young officer of yours who drives a 1946 Ford coupé would get involved in a drunken brawl with several men at The Red Wheel. Even though this trooper was in civilian clothes I think it's a disgrace to your organisation. How long will this type of thing go on? If something drastic isn't done I will release all this news to all the newspapers.

Patriotic Observer.

When I finished reading the letter, Captain Dondera

was holding his hand out for it. I passed it over to him.

"I'm waiting for an explanation," he said. His voice was impersonal. Dondera had a reputation for poise and affability. He was often a speaker at clubs and luncheons, lecturing on police matters and civic responsibility. But this was another Dondera talking, the hard-bitten troop commander in his strictly-business voice. A seasoned cop with a mind tuned to suspicion and distrust.

"It's a big exaggeration, Captain," I said.

"Is that all you have to say?" he asked, granite-faced. "An exaggeration?"

"No, sir," I said. Then I explained to him what had happened at The Red Wheel. He listened with an alert, wary expression on his face.

"So you were in there cadging free drinks," he said. "What were you going to give Podre in return?"

"Nothing. It wasn't anything like that."

"A man sets up free drinks for a cop," Dondera said, watching my face closely, "he expects favours back. Don't kid yourself, Lindsey. You're not *that* naïve."

"I'm not trying to kid myself. It was only one drink and I saw nothing wrong with it. I've known Carl Podre a long time. He came from my neighbourhood. I had been friendly with his kid brother. If Carl invited me into his house for a drink, nobody would have thought that was wrong. I figure this is the same thing. He wasn't trying to buy anything, and I wasn't in uniform."

"The uniform has nothing to do with it. You got into a fight with some drunks in a public place. I'm a reasonable man, Lindsey. I don't mind my troopers having a ball once in a while. But on the quiet. Let 'em go off somewhere out of sight where I don't hear about it."

" It wasn't a fight, Captain. I just removed one man from the premises."

" Because he made a few remarks about a night-club singer. What were you acting as, the official bouncer for The Red Wheel? "

" No, sir."

" You know the regulations about conduct in a public place."

" Yes, sir."

" You keep getting tangled up here, Lindsey. I'd like to know who is making all this trouble for you."

" So would I, sir."

" I don't like the way this looks, Lindsey. We've had men who were accident-prone. You put them in a cruiser and they crack it up. Put them on a motor-cycle and they break a collarbone. Accident-prone, no matter what kind of an assignment you give them. They may have the best intentions in the world but you have to ease them out of the organisation. You're the same way. It's never your fault, but you keep getting jammed up all the time. And, what's more important, I don't want a man in my troop who keeps making mistakes in judgment."

He looked at me, waiting for an answer. I didn't have one.

" I'm sorry, Lindsey," he said. " I'm more sorry for your father because I have a lot of respect for him. But I'll have to turn this over to Major Carradine. Meanwhile you'll make out a complete report on it. Understand? "

"Yes, Captain."

"I don't know if they'll suspend you or not pending the investigation. I'll leave it entirely up to them."

He dismissed me abruptly. I went out of the duty office, past the dining-room, where I heard the clatter of dishes and glassware, and up the stairs to my room. I lay back on the royal blue blanket and stared up at the ceiling. Captain Dondera had made his point. A trooper, off duty, had no business being in a place where rough and abusive language was used. If he did go into such a place by mistake with his wife or girl friend, he was supposed to leave quickly and quietly.

I lit a cigarette and inhaled the smoke, thinking, bitterly, they expected too much from you. Lead the life of a celibate monk. Keep away from bars and trouble spots. Don't defend your girl. Don't have too many drinks. Go to a movie and hold hands, or sit in a living-room and play anagrams.

And I knew what would happen next. The executive officer, Major Carradine, would make Captain-Adjutant Crow aware of it, then turn the matter over to Divisional Inspector Reilly for investigation. While that was in process the trooper was usually transferred to another barracks. The investigation could result in one of two things. A suspension with loss of pay, or loss of time off for a specified period. I didn't think it was serious enough to warrant a court-martial or my resignation.

The worst part was thinking of how my father would take it. He would know about it soon enough, and my future career would be as clear as rain to him.

I was down to the end of my cigarette when I heard somebody coming up the stairs. Tony Pellegrini poked his head into the doorway and said, " What's the matter, kid? No chow? "

" I had something on the road," I lied. I was choked up and I tried hard not to show it. I don't know if I was deceiving him. As much as these little matters were hushed up they had a way of getting around the barracks.

" You riding with Ludwell again to-night? " Pellegrini asked.

" I don't know," I said.

Pellegrini leaned against the door jamb. " How do you like Ludwell? "

" Okay."

He nodded, then grinned. " Look kid, you might find it a little tough here at first. They hold a tight rein on you."

" I've been finding that out, Tony."

" Stay with it. Just clamp your teeth and hang on tight. It'll pass."

" I hope so."

He locked his thumbs in his gunbelt. " You remember asking me about shapers? "

" Sure," I said.

" Did you have any particular reason for asking me? "

" No, Tony."

" You're sure, kid? "

" Yes. Why? "

" Nothing." He stood there for moment as though bursting to say something. I knew he would never say it. He scraped a toe on the floor and fiddled with his gunbelt. " Look," he said, " any time you've got a problem and you want to talk about it. I'm around.

I might not pull any weight around here, but I'm a good listener, kid."

" Thanks, Tony."

He waved his hand. " I'll see you later. If you want me, I'll be out on Route 1 chasing tail-lights."

He left. I stood up and went to the bureau. On it was the blackened brooch. I picked it up and looked at it. Then I went over to Keith Ludwell's special silver polish.

I cleaned the brooch, being especially careful with the fine strands of the cobweb. When I was through it shone. I looked at the initials on the back. A.B. Amy Bell. It could be nobody else.

I wrapped the silver cobweb in a piece of tissue and put it into my drawer.

CHAPTER FIFTEEN

SERGEANT NEAL didn't send me out on patrol that night. Keith Ludwell drove off with Driscoll and I was assigned to other duties. First I drove a cruiser to the Framingham troop headquarters garage for servicing and repairs, leaving it there and returning with another. Then I went on a mail delivery, meeting an Andover cruiser near Georgetown and swapping parcels. When I got back to the barracks I had a great deal of paper work to do. It gave me a chance to check the files. There were no major crimes last summer when Amy Bell had first arrived in Dorset. I asked Sergeant Neal if anything unusual had happened about that time.

"I don't remember anything special," he said. "Just regular small stuff. Why?"

"No big robberies or anything?"

"No," he said. "Why do you ask?"

"Nothing," I said. I handed the papers to him. "I'm finished with these reports."

I went upstairs, cleaned and oiled my gun and polished all my leather and buttons. I got my laundry together. When I finished it was midnight. Sergeant Neal told me I could turn in.

The next morning, Saturday, they sent me out to assist Chief Rigsby again. I drove down to Rigsby's garage on Main Street. He was working on a car that was set up on jacks. Crawling out from under the car, he wiped a smear of grease from his cheek.

"You're back again," he said. "What are we supposed to do together?"

"I don't know," I said. "They sent me here. There's no reason why we can't do a good, careful investigation."

"We've tried our best, haven't we?" he asked. "What else is there we can do?"

"We might have missed something."

He took out a battered pack of cigarettes and offered me one. I lit up. The cigarette had no taste. Breakfast had had no taste. I was a little heart-sick about everything.

"I'm surprised Bart Neal is paying so much attention to me," Rigsby said. "I've got no police force, no radio, no police car. I'm nothing more than a part-time night watchman." He wet the end of his cigarette, put it in his mouth and lit it. "Now if I had an organisation like Marblehead or Newburyport or Gloucester it would be different."

" Size isn't everything," I said.

" I'm nothing, Lindsey. Your boys don't have any use for me and I don't blame them."

" No, they've got a lot of respect for you."

He sat down on a workbench and smoked. " I guess I should be doing something. I can't just sit around, putting in my time and waiting, can I? "

" No," I said. " Because you're closer to it than anybody else."

" I don't have anything to work with, Lindsey. I don't have what your outfit has. They've got everything."

" You've got one thing they haven't got. You're closest to it. You could spot something they might have missed."

" It's no good to be too close to it. Sometimes it affects your reasoning."

" Why? " I asked.

" Because I'm not thinking of Swenke. I'm thinking of Mary Ann Fedder. I remember her since she was five years old and she was going to church in a starched pink dress and a straw bonnet with ribbons on it. In her hand she had a nickel because she wanted to put her own money in the collection plate. Those are the things I remember——" He broke off, dropped the cigarette and ground it hard under his heel. " I knew Mary Ann. She would never do anything wrong. She'd never get mixed up with a Swenke—not intentionally."

" There was a suitcase in her car," I said.

" I don't care about the suitcase. I knew Mary Ann, I tell you."

" So we try a new direction."

" Sure," he said. He waved his hand. " North, east, south, west. She went somewhere Tuesday afternoon. She crossed paths with Swenke for the first time. I'm sure of that, and that's all I'm sure of. Thursday Russell Westlake disappears. There's another kid I'd stake my life on. Could I be that far wrong? All these years living in this town, wouldn't I know those two kids? "

" Sure, you would."

" So now it's your turn, Ralph. They spent a lot of money training you. You're supposed to be smart and alert."

" Supposed to be." I said.

" All right," he said. " Where did Mary Ann go? How did she meet Swenke and what was he doing at the time? "

" I've got my mind set on one thing," I said. " I keep thinking of their honeymoon plans. There must have been some rumours around where these kids were going to honeymoon."

" We went over that," he said, his shoulders drooping tiredly. " There was nothing. It was all a big secret."

" Why? Why should a honeymoon be such a big secret? "

" Don't ask me," Rigsby said. " I never had a honeymoon. I got married in the service on a three-day pass."

" These kids were trying to save money. If I was trying to save money I'd get a cottage somewhere. This time of year it would be dirt cheap."

" To each his own," Rigsby said. " If it was me I'd sure take in Bermuda."

" Bermuda would cost money. A summer cottage in the month of May or June would be a lot cheaper."

He moved off the bench and stood there pinching his ear. " Would you go back there, Ralph? "

" Go where? "

" Say you were Russell Westlake and you rented a honeymoon cottage. Then your girl was murdered. Would you ever go back to the cottage again? "

" That's what I've been thinking about," I said. " Would *you* go back? "

" Not me. I wouldn't want to see it ever again. I wouldn't even want to think about it."

" *I* might," I said slowly. " I might be sentimental. I might want to go there and dream a little and picture myself there with my bride."

" Romance stuff. That's because you're younger than I."

" So is Russell Westlake, remember. I'm trying to think like he would."

" It would be like pulling out your own teeth."

" Not necessarily. It could be dream stuff. Some people live on that kind of thing. A man like Russell Westlake might do it, Chief."

" Al," he said. " Call me Al. I'm a hell of a chief. I've heard the selectmen are going to give me the can."

" Because of one murder? "

" The first murder they ever had in this town. A cop is hired to prevent crime. I didn't prevent this one. So I have to take the rap. They throw me out and put in another chief. Then everybody is happy."

" I don't get it," I said. " It wasn't your fault."

" Since when does it count whose fault it is? The

world is made up of wolves and goats. I'm a goat."

"Dammit, it's not right."

"What are you getting so stirred up about? Did you ever squawk when a baseball club fired a manager? He might have all .250 banjo hitters and ten sore-armed old pitchers. The team's in last place. The public screams for somebody's scalp. What do the owners do? They fire the manager. Then everybody's satisfied. They start coming back to the ball park. Of course, the team doesn't get any better. You still have the .250 hitters and the sore-armed pitchers. So the team ends up in last place again. What happens? They fire that manager and get a new one. And so it goes, on and on. Every time the wolves howl they sacrifice a goat."

"You don't have to be a goat," I said.

"Sure, I can always fix cars."

"No, you can crack this case, Al."

"With what? If the case is going to be cracked, the State Police will do it, not me."

"But with your help," I said. "You've got one thing I haven't got. Local knowledge."

"Knowledge. A hell of a lot of knowledge I've got. I wouldn't know if my coat was on fire."

"You've got a bad fault, Al. You keep running yourself down. Snap out of it and let's think about the possible honeymoon cottage again. Maybe those kids had a friend who owns a summer cottage and would let them use it."

Rigsby shook his head. "The honeymoon plans were a secret. If a friend knew, it would let the cat out of the bag. Anyway, your own cops have contacted all friends."

" All right, what about the Fedders? If they owned a cottage, Mary Ann could get the key without anyone being the wiser."

" They don't have a cottage. But come again."

" The Westlakes."

" No. They did own a cottage. Not any more. They sold it last year."

" You're sure? "

" Yes."

" Wait a minute," I said. " Where was the cottage? In Ipswich? "

" Why did you pick Ipswich? "

" Everything keeps pointing to Ipswich. Westlake's car was found in Ipswich. Was their cottage in Ipswich? "

" No. It was on Dorset Pond."

" So we'll change direction," I said. " Dorset Pond. Who bought the Westlake cottage? "

Rigsby pulled at his ear. " Somebody in Groveland named Henry Allenby." He fished for a cigarette and looked at it thoughtfully before putting it in his mouth. " What do you think? "

" That could be it," I said. " Don't you see the gag? The big joke? The secret? Westlake spends his honeymoon at his old family cottage. Nobody would think he'd rent it from Allenby."

" It's a chance. But you could be wrong."

" I've got a terrific knack of being wrong," I said. " But all it takes is one phone call. I'll pay for it."

" It's on me. Use mine in the office."

I went into his tiny office, called Groveland and spoke to some woman at the Allenby house. Then a man came on the phone. I told him it was the State Police calling.

"I'm inquiring about that cottage you bought from the Westlakes last year," I said.

"I don't see where I have to give back the money," Allenby said. "It ain't my fault the girl was killed. They rented the cottage for a week and they can have it. A deal is a deal. As it is, I let them have it dirt cheap. The law can't force me to give back the twenty dollars."

"Mr. Allenby," I said, "I don't give a damn about the twenty dollars. I want to know if you rented the cottage to Russell Westlake."

"I did. And a deal's a deal."

"Have you seen Russell since you rented the cottage to him?"

"No. I ain't seen him in a month. And it won't do him no good to try and get the twenty dollars back."

"Did you give him a key, sir?"

"Didn't have to. There's only one key. It's always kept under the milk box on the front porch. If Russell's gone and lost that key I'll charge him for making another. I paid his family a good price for that cottage."

"Good-bye, sir," I said. I hung up.

Coming out of the office I saw Chief Rigsby washing his hands at the sink.

"Well?" he said. "Any luck?"

"We've made a start," I said. "Russell did rent the cottage from Allenby. From the way Allenby talks, I guess he doesn't know Russell has disappeared."

Rigsby put on his leather jacket. "You coming out to the pond with me to have a look at it?"

" I sure am."

He was buckling an old holstered Colt revolver under his jacket. " Are you going to call your barracks and tell them? "

" Yes," I said. " But I don't think they care much where I go or what I do."

" Oh," he said. Then after a moment, " You're on the out-list, too? "

" Way down at the bottom, Al. You're looking at one of those goats. They're going to transfer me out of here."

" I'm sorry," he said. " You make me feel ashamed of myself, kid."

" Why? "

" A youngster like you, you've been listening to all my whining without saying a word. All the time you had your own troubles."

" Forget it," I said. " Do you want to take both cars? "

" It would be better. If anything comes up, we may need both."

" Fine," I said. " I'll follow you."

I went outside to the cruiser, called Corporal Kerrigan on the radio and told him where I was going with Chief Rigsby. He said to go ahead, and he wished me luck, and from the tone of his voice I think he knew I needed it.

CHAPTER SIXTEEN

I FOLLOWED the old Pontiac down Pond Road, passing the Derechy house. The two children, filthy and grimy, were playing in a trash pile near Derechy's old hulk of a car.

We made the turn at the pond and rode up over the bluff. My heart gave a little thump as we passed the parking area where I had been with Amy Bell. That was another interlude that seemed over, too.

The Pontiac descended slowly along the twin ruts. I followed, passing the spot where I had found the silver brooch. The Pontiac bumped and groaned as we came through the overhang of fir trees and into the dappled sunlight of a grove. To the left was the cottage covered with boiler plating over the windows. Another boarded cottage was to the right.

Rigsby continued across the grove another fifty yards. Nestled in the pines was a white clapboard bungalow with red trim. He stopped. I pulled up behind him and shut off the motor.

My shoes crunched on the brown pine needles as I joined him in front of the little screened porch. I looked down at the ground, seeing the outline of tyre marks. Above us a stray puff of wind sighed through the trees, and beyond us the waters of the pond rippled in a narrow streak as the wind moved across it. There was a sharp fragrance of pine.

I walked around the cottage with Rigsby and tried to look into the windows. They were covered with blue shades.

We stepped up on to the screened porch and tried the front door. It was locked. Rigsby looked at me, pulling at his ear.

" You forgot to get permission to go inside," he said.

I moved the green wooden milk box aside. Under it, on the floor, was the key. I picked it up. " From what I know of Allenby he'd charge us an admission fee," I said. " If there's a rap for illegal entry, I'll take it. One more mark on my report won't matter."

I turned the key in the lock and opened the door. The place had a dead, airless, musty smell. Near the door were two fabric suitcases and some fishing tackle. A .22 calibre rifle stood in a corner. I didn't touch the rifle, but went over, bent and sniffed at the muzzle. There was an odour of oil and metal, not of gunpowder.

I crossed the living-room and went into the kitchen. The cupboards held several cans of food and the storage area under the sink had kitchen utensils. The icebox was empty. Leaving there I went into the bedroom and looked around. There was nothing in the closet. The mattress on the big double bed was rolled. I went into a second bedroom. Same thing.

Back in the living-room I said to Rigsby, " What do you think, Al? Can you identify the luggage? "

" No," Rigsby said. " But it figures. It must belong to the kids."

" And where does Whitey Swenke come into it? "

" I don't know," Rigsby said. " If I was going to give it a fast shuffle I'd come up with the story that Swenke, by coincidence, was using this cottage as a hide-out. When Mary Ann Fedder came here Tuesday, to bring a suitcase, she walked in on Swenke.

Swenke chased her all the way home and killed her."

" Only that's all wrong," I said.

" Of course it's wrong. You can see the kids made more than one visit to bring things. They would have known on their first visit that Swenke was hiding here. Second, Swenke wasn't identified in the Newburyport robbery. He still hasn't been. He's been popping up in Boston. He was seen there at a ball game, and Tuesday morning he was there to rent a truck. So, to me, it doesn't make sense that Swenke was hiding out at all. Not in a remote spot like this. Where does that lead us to, kid? "

" To Russell Westlake," I said. " Do you think he's been back here since the murder? "

" You're the expert," Rigsby said. " Take a look at those tyre marks outside."

" I saw them," I said. " They're too faint. How about looking at that .22 rifle and telling me if it's Westlake's? "

" It might be. It's a Remington repeater and Russell owns a Remington repeater. But so do a lot of other people."

" We do know one thing," I said. " Russell West-lake was angry. He was out gunning for somebody. Maybe the first time Russell Westlake was here he didn't bring the rifle. Maybe he brought it with him the last time——" I stopped.

" Well? " Rigsby asked.

I shook my head. " It's no good to keep saying 'maybe,' Al. Maybe's don't make facts. We need more than theories."

" There's one way to find out," Rigsby said. " Let's

E

go back to town and get the Fedders and the West-lakes. They can identify all this stuff."

" You go, Al," I said. " I'll have to stay here and guard the evidence."

" That's right," he said. " I'm learning something all the time. You'll make a cop out of me yet, kid."

I went outside with him and watched him drive away. Then I walked over to my cruiser, warmed up the radio and signalled the barracks. Corporal Kerrigan came on. I told him what we had found.

" Stand by and I'll meet you there myself," Kerrigan said. " Everybody else is out on the investigation in Ipswich. K2 off."

I heard him give a Signal 7 to Cruiser 28, which meant Trooper Doherty would come into the barracks to take over the desk.

I hung up the handphone and shut off the radio. The wind had died down and had left an uncanny, eerie quietness in the grove. The trees were motionless.

I closed the car door and looked at the little white cabin. A honeymoon cottage for two young people about to start life together. But it was ended before it started. The girl was dead and the boy had dis-appeared. It was cruel and wrong.

There was something else wrong with the picture. I couldn't put my finger on it. All I knew was that something material was missing. Something didn't fit.

I stepped up on the porch, looked around at the milk box and the wire screening, at the floor boards, at the windows, at the front door. It wasn't there.

I went inside. In the living-room I looked at the

luggage, the fishing equipment, the .22 rifle. It wasn't there, either.

Into the kitchen. I looked around, staring at the cupboards, the old black-slate sink, the old icebox, the four chairs and the porcelain-topped table. I kept turning around, circling. Something was wrong in the kitchen. The picture didn't jell. It wasn't instinct, or a sixth sense, or anything extra-sensory. It was something pertaining to the eye, to vision.

I started at one end of the kitchen. The old icebox, yellowish with age, typical summer camp equipment. It was empty and clean. The wooden cupboards. Old and a little warped. Nothing wrong there. The sink. A cheap black-slate affair with two faucets. Ancient and out-dated. A fifty-gallon galvanised hot-water tank. I touched it. It was cold. Standard equipment. Four wooden chairs and a wooden, porcelain-topped table. Something else was missing.

A cooking stove.

There was no stove in the kitchen. Not even an electric hot-plate or an oil-burning job. No stove at all.

There was a space for a stove between the sink and the icebox. I bent down and looked. Black soot on the floor. My eyes came up, searching the wall. There was a circular hole where the flue had been. Soot had dribbled down and had stained the white wall.

I sank to my haunches and examined the floor. There were four indentations where the legs of the stove had rested. There were also scraping marks across the floor as though the stove had been dragged away. I stood up and followed the marks to the back door. There I stopped.

So what, I thought. The Westlakes had sold the cottage to Henry Allenby and the stove wasn't part of the deal. Or the stove was old and broken and Allenby had thrown it out.

But there could be still another reason for the disappearance of the stove. The stove was a heavy one and it had had to be dragged. And a heavy stove could be used as a weight. And a weight could be tied to a dead body. And the weight and the dead body could be dropped into the pond so that they both disappeared.

Which led to the final conclusion. Russell Westlake had been murdered and his body was at the bottom of Dorset Pond.

CHAPTER SEVENTEEN

THE BACK DOOR of the cottage was latched from the inside with a sliding bolt. It was stiff but I worked it open. Outside was a tiny open porch. Beyond the porch was an open field filled with high weeds. The weeds were matted in a narrow swath. I followed the swath about fifteen feet. To the right my eye caught something black in the underbrush. I went over. It was the discarded flue from the stove.

I didn't touch it. I went back and followed the curving swath a few more feet. The swath ended in the pine needles at the edge of the grove. No sign of the stove. It had been dragged to this point and no farther.

I bent down and examined the soil and the pine

needles. Faint tyre tracks, deeper at the edge of the
bushes, as though a car or truck had been backed in
there and the stove had been lifted on to it.

I straightened up. Perhaps I was making too much
of it, I thought. The stove could have been no good
and had probably been picked up and taken away by
a junk dealer. Because if it was to be used to sink a
body in the pond, there was no sense in putting the
stove into a truck.

Or perhaps there *was* sense to it. It would be easier to
put the stove into a vehicle to get it down to the water.

I walked, following the tyre tracks across the pine
needles. They curved away from the cottage, then
went thirty yards down a gradual slope to the narrow
sandy shore of the pond. I stopped. Here the tracks
had been smoothed out and carefully obliterated.

The beach was of firm, hard-packed, yellow-brown
sand. Along the shore the water was clear and shallow.
I walked along, first to the left, following the beach
to where it ended in a soft marsh and a cluster of
floating lily pads. Nothing.

Turning, I walked back, eyeing the sun-glinted water.
I could see nothing except a wooden float and diving
board about forty feet out. I continued along until
the beach ended on the right at a steep, eroded bluff.

I stood there for a moment in the dead stillness.
There was no doubt in my mind any more. The truck
or car that had carried the stove had come to the edge
of the water. If the stove was a heavy one it could
not have been dragged far into the pond. I would have
been able to see it from where I was standing. Unless
it had been lifted into a boat.

But what kind of boat? It was not a large pond

and there was no sign of any boats around. Also, a heavy bulky stove might capsize an ordinary rowboat or sailboat.

What else? Observe. Take in everything. Nothing on the beach except the sand and my own footsteps. Nothing on the water except the float forty feet out. A grey-painted float with a canvas-topped springboard, buoyed up by large empty steel drums.

It was the float, of course. They could disengage the float, bring it to shore and lift the stove and body on to it. Next, paddle the float out into the pond, tie the body to the stove and drop them both off the side. Then paddle the float back, anchor it again, and swim to shore.

I stood there looking at the float as it lay there almost motionless on the still blue water. I took out my pack of cigarettes and lit one. I was thinking of how to follow through. I had no boat. And, although, at the Academy, the swimming tests and life-saving instruction had been rigid enough, I couldn't very well leave my uniform and weapon on the shore and start swimming around the pond.

I took one puff of the cigarette and ground it impatiently into the sand. Elevation was what I needed. The Coast Guard used helicopters to spot contraband dropped into the ocean offshore. A good high tree might do it.

I walked along the beach to the bluff. At the top of it was a stand of high pine trees. I climbed the bluff into the clump of pines, looked up and picked the tallest and sturdiest. I leaped up, swung on to a branch and started climbing. The branches were resinous, and shreds of bark and gobs of sap began sticking to my hands.

I climbed higher. The tree swayed under my weight. About two-thirds up, the tree began to bend ominously. I halted.

Looking down across the pond I saw that the sand extended out from the shore about twenty feet. From there the bottom of the pond darkened. The water was clear enough. I could see green reeds and ferns on the pond bed. But a black stove—if it was black—would be hard to spot. The idea was not to look for the stove but for the body.

I saw it. The white shirt was what attracted me. The body was ten or fifteen feet out from where the float was anchored. It startled me for a moment, prickling the hair on the nape of my neck. Because I could have sworn that it was alive. The head was down and the legs were widespread and the arms seemed to be moving as though the body were swimming under water. It was due, of course, to the light refraction in the water and the currents of the pond. I couldn't see the stove. Its colour was blended into the darkness of the pond bottom.

So there it was, I thought. First, Mary Ann Fedder coming out to the cottage to bring some clothes in a suitcase. The poor kid had seen something she shouldn't have seen. Something in the grove or around the cottage near it. She had run and she had been chased home by Kurt Swenke, and, as she was phoning the police, Swenke had broken in and shot her down.

Then Russell Westlake had gone out to the cottage, whether to pick up his possessions, or to scout around for the reason of Mary Ann's death, or for a dreamlike reverie, and he had seen the same thing. But they had caught Westlake before he could make his move. He had been killed, tied to the old stove and dumped into the pond. His car had been driven away and abandoned in Ipswich.

But Kurt Swenke had not killed Russell Westlake. Swenke was in jail. There was somebody else.

Holding on to the tree-trunk I scanned the waters again, looking across the pond to the opposite shore, to the little piers jutting out from tiny, sandy beaches, to varicoloured cabins, all shuttered and seemingly uninhabited. Then back again to my own side of the shore, scanning first to the right and seeing nothing but the occasional roof of a cabin through the trees. To the left now. And fifty feet away, in a clump of bushes, I saw something move. My eyes riveted down, picking out a patch of yellow cloth. Then a man's head.

Somebody had been watching me.

I began to edge down the tree-trunk. The bushes swayed and the man began to slither away.

" Hold it," I shouted. " You there, stop."

The yellow shirt froze. Now it burrowed deeper into the bushes until I could only see a sliver of colour. The sun glinted on dull metal.

A bullet ricocheted off a tree-trunk near me. As it screamed away I heard the echoing boom of the shot. A rifle, from the sound of it.

Is quirmed around to the back of the tree-trunk, one leg braced against a branch, the other suspended awkwardly in mid-air. I held on to the trunk with one hand, and my fingers opened my holster flap and brought out the long-barrelled service revolver.

I was clumsy with the revolver. My position was strained and my hands were sticky with pine gum. I tried to get a better grip on the revolver butt and, as I did, it slipped out of my fingers. The revolver bounced once on a branch and made a parabola to the ground.

I looked down. The gun had disappeared in the underbrush somewhere fifteen feet below me. I clung to the trunk and cursed myself steadily for three seconds. In my black gunbelt was a leather cartridge pouch that contained twenty-four rounds of ammunition. In my leather handcuff case was a pair of shiny bracelets. On my whistle chain were my whistle and handcuff key. In my hip pocket I carried a billy. Fully equipped. Only without my revolver.

I edged down the trunk. The second shot came. It smacked into the trunk about the level of my eyes, splintering the wood and vibrating the tree with its impact. I froze there. A high-powered rifle, I thought. And he was getting the range.

I felt like a sitting duck in a shooting gallery. My light blue blouse and the broad, light blue stripe down the side of my breeches made a good target for him. Sweat began to trickle from my forehead and my armpits grew wet. One thing I couldn't understand. Whoever the sharpshooter was, he had a chance to get away. But, apparently, he was satisfied to lie there in the bushes and try to kill me.

I wanted to stay there behind the solid wood of the tree-trunk. But the trunk was narrow and offered only partial protection and my uniform was not the camouflage suit of an Army sniper. I had to move down.

I slid to the branch below me. The rifle fired again. Two shots, both ripping bark from the tree, one bullet so close that it flipped my sleeve as it went by.

I jumped. It was a long drop and I fell heavily into the bushes, scratching my face and jarring my left arm to the shoulder socket. I fished desperately for my revolver, finding it, grabbing it and cocking the hammer. I turned now to face the man. I couldn't find him.

A shot broke the stillness of the air, echoing across the water. I flinched instinctively, but this time there was no bullet past my head. The crack had come some distance from my left, from the direction of the road.

My head swivelled. I saw a flash of light blue colour. A trooper was running along the edge of the grove toward a clump of bushes, zigzagging through the trees, a Winchester .30-.30 in his hands.

It was Corporal Phil Kerrigan. A rifle shot answered him from the right. Kerrigan stopped behind a tree, took aim and pumped five shots rapid-fire at the clump of bushes. As he did, I broke out of the underbrush and ran forward into the grove.

Kerrigan saw me and shouted, " You all right, Ralph? "

" Fine," I called back. I looked towards the bushes. I couldn't see the yellow shirt. The angle of vision was different at ground level.

" Where is he? " I called to Kerrigan.

" He's still in there," Kerrigan said, pointing. " Circle around to the right so you cut him off. I'll move in."

I began to circle. Kerrigan ran forward to another

tree, his black, shiny boots flashing in the dappled sunlight. I bent low, ran across an open spot and ducked behind a tree.

Kerrigan moved again, coming closer, his rifle aimed at the bushes. There was no movement in there. I peered out from behind my tree, my revolver levelled. No movement yet. I ran to the next tree. Now I saw a patch of yellow. The man was still there.

" Come out," I called to him.

There was no answer. I looked across at Kerrigan. He was silent for a moment. Then he said, " I'm going in. Cover me, kid."

He had to walk across open ground now. I kept my revolver aimed at the clump of bushes, waiting for the slightest stir. Kerrigan walked steadily, his rifle barrel fixed on the bushes.

He came on to them and waded through. Then he stopped short, turned and waved to me. I came running.

The man lay on his side, his mouth and eyes open, a deep furrow along the side of his skull near the hair-line, blood seeping from it. Another bullet had ploughed across the top of his head, taking part of the skull with it. The blood had run down his face and was dripping to the ground.

With his boot, Kerrigan pushed away the man's rifle. Then he bent down feeling for a heartbeat.

He stood up and looked at me. " Stone cold dead." His hand trembled on his own rifle. I knew why, too. He had just killed a man and it would stay with him a long time.

I looked at the man's face. It had at least a week's growth of beard on it, but it was vaguely familiar to me, as though I had seen a picture of him before. The yellow shirt was soiled and covered with blood.

"Who is he?" I asked.

"George 'Slicker' Hozak," Kerrigan said, his eyes in pain.

"The Newburyport bank job?"

"That's it. Hozak, the brains of the outfit."

"He had guts, too," I said. "I'll grant him that much. He could have run. But he didn't. He stayed and shot it out."

"He couldn't run," Kerrigan said tonelessly. "He was cornered like a rat, so he had to fight like a rat. Look and see, kid."

I looked down at the body and saw what Kerrigan meant. Hozak's right leg, partially covered with his left, had a crude wooden splint running from hip to ankle. The bandage wrapped around the splint was muddy and caked with pus. For the first time now, I was aware of a stench coming from it. Gangrene. Once, in Korea on patrol, I had come across a wounded R.O.K. soldier. He had lain there for several days and he had smelled the same way.

"My guess is it's a femur wound," Kerrigan said. "His thigh was in rotten shape." A big, bluebottle fly buzzed over the body and landed on Hozak's face. Kerrigan brushed at it absently, then fixed his eyes on me. "How did the shooting start?"

"He spotted me up in a tree," I said.

Kerrigan said, "A tree? What the hell were you doing up in a tree?"

I smiled wanly. "It's a long story. But I think Russell Westlake is dead." I pointed to the pond. "His body's in the drink."

" You've seen it? "

" From the tree," I said. " There's a body out there and I think it's Westlake's."

Kerrigan set the safety lock on the Winchester. " I heard rifle shots when I came in. I saw your cruiser but I didn't see you. Hozak was shooting but you weren't shooting back. What happened? "

" That's another long story, Phil. You see, I was—"

" If it's such a long story," Kerrigan said, " I'd better go and radio the bigwigs first. Then you can tell me."

CHAPTER EIGHTEEN

THEY BROUGHT the body up out of Dorset Pond. It was Russell Westlake's and it was tied to an old black, cast-iron stove. Later, Ballistics said he had been killed by bullets from Hozak's rifle. The medical examiner's autopsy showed Westlake was already dead when he entered the water.

The luggage in the little cottage was identified as belonging to Mary Ann Fedder and Russell Westlake. The .22 Remington rifle had not been fired recently and that had belonged to Russell Westlake, too.

Meanwhile, even before the big brass came, we had begun a search of all the camps in the area. We didn't have to look far. The camp Hozak had been using for a hide-out was the one across the grove that had boiler plating covering the windows. Inside there was a bad stench of blood and decay, old pus-stained bandages, empty penicillin bottles, empty cans of food, empty whisky bottles and many flies. But there was no money from the Newburyport robbery.

Throughout the day we went from cottage to cottage around the pond, searching for further evidence, for other signs of occupancy, for witnesses. We found none.

It was about eight o'clock in the evening when I came back to the barracks. Detective-Lieutenant Ed Newpole was waiting in the guardroom for me. He took notes as I related everything that had happened that morning. I left nothing out either. When I came to the part about dropping my revolver from the tree, his hand poised with the pen for a moment and a little glint came to his eyes, but he said not a word.

When I was finished he put the pen down and brought out a pipe. " You and Rigsby did some good thinking," he said. " It's the kind of thinking old Walt would have done."

" Thanks," I said. He always called my father " old Walt " even though he and my father were about the same age.

" You'll have to make out a full report of your own," Newpole said, tamping tobacco into his pipe. " I might as well fill in some of the background for you."

" Yes, sir," I said.

" We don't have any eyewitnesses," he said, " so we'll have to plug along with what evidence we have. The few missing parts we'll have to fill in with ideas of our own. It's quite a case."

He lit the pipe, puffed on it, then sank back in his chair. " It starts, of course, with the bank robbery in Newburyport. A well-planned job. Any Hozak job is well-planned. Small gang. Three men. One hitch, though. A minor car accident on Water Street. The Newburyport foot patrolman investigating the accident is a few minutes late for lunch. So he shows up and takes some shots as the men are breaking from the bank. That's where Hozak himself got it in the thigh. The others dragged him into the car and they sped away.

" Next the alarm went out and all highways in the radius were blocked. But the Hozak plan was good. They had a hide-out, not in Ipswich where they've tried to decoy us, but in Dorset. Why did they pick Dorset? Because it was close by and because Dorset is a one-cop town and has no police radio. So the men turned off before they hit the roadblocks, went through Dorset and holed up at Dorset Pond. Safe enough for a little while. None of those cabins would be opened for a month. By that time they would split up and take off one by one.

" Yes, a good plan. But there was a second hitch. Hozak was wounded more than they thought. He couldn't be moved. So they bound him up the best they could and waited for him to get better. He didn't. The leg got worse and they knew they had to get him out of there and to a doctor. So Swenke went to Boston and made arrangements to rent a truck. In it they were going to transport Hozak. I don't know where. These thugs always have a doctor they own."

Newpole drew on the pipe and looked at me. " Now Mary Ann Fedder comes into the picture. She and Westlake have rented the cottage across from Hozak's for their honeymoon. They come there with their luggage and drop it off. Cute, funny little secret. Poor kids. Nobody knows they're going to honeymoon only five miles away from Main Street. Nobody knows but Hozak who's looking out through the boiler plating, watching them and getting badly frightened about it. So he tells Swenke and Swenke hurries back that afternoon with the truck. Swenke goes into the hide-out cottage and drags out Hozak." Newpole put his pipe down. "You understand that this part of it is only guesswork. We have to fill it in the best way we can."

"Yes, sir," I said. "But it sounds logical."

"All right," Newpole said. "Just as Swenke is carrying Hozak out, Mary Ann drives into the grove, bringing a suitcase. She sees Swenke and Hozak, gets scared, turns her car around and drives off. Swenke drops Hozak and goes after her. If she gets to a phone, everything is all over. So he chases her into Dorset and kills her as she's phoning the barracks. When Swenke drives away he's heading back towards the pond. He never gets there. You capture him. Hozak is still out at the cottage, helpless. Swenke is in jail as quiet as a man with a talkative wife and a tough mother-in-law.

"Now Russell Westlake comes into the picture. What was in his mind we'll never find out. But we do know now he had withheld information from us. He had one trump card we didn't have—knowledge of the honeymoon cottage. For whatever reason he had, he came to the pond. The poor lad may have thought he was being an avenging angel. He might have gone back just to retrieve his things. He might have gone there to take the law in his own hands. We'll never know. Revenge does terrible things to people. Anyway, he drives out to the grove. There's a spot beside the Hozak cottage with an old mattress on the ground. We think Hozak used it for getting some sun. Westlake spots Hozak or Hozak spots him. Whichever it was, Hozak shoots and kills Westlake. The body is then tied to a stove, brought out to the middle of the pond and dumped. Then Westlake's car is driven to the state forest in Ipswich and abandoned. That's our story. Only there's a big hitch in our story, too."

"Yes, sir," I said.

He smiled broadly. "Where, son?"

"There were three men in all this," I said. "Not just Swenke and Hozak. Three men pulled the robbery. Ordinarily, the third man could have been in South America by now. But he wasn't. When it came to Westlake's murder, Swenke was in jail and Hozak was badly wounded. Hozak couldn't have handled Westlake's body. He couldn't drive West-lake's car to Ipswich. The third man is still around, Lieutenant."

"Yes," Newpole said. "We want the third man. A man strong enough to handle a heavy stove. A local man."

"Why local?"

"The hide-away cottage, the one with the boiler plating. It doesn't belong to anybody who lives around here. It belongs to a former Haverhill man who's a small shoe-manufacturer. A year ago last spring, he moved his factory to Knoxville, Tennessee. His cottage has been empty since. No danger of anyone coming there. Only a local person would know that."

"Yes," I said. "A man named Joe Derechy."

"How do you figure Derechy, Ralph?"

"Because he lives in a cottage near the pond. A

perfect lookout spot for the gang. He'd see all the traffic going back and forth. It would be unusual this time of year and, unless he was in on the deal, he'd mention it to Chief Rigsby. And I remember asking Derechy when I was checking the area. Although he had been all through there picking wood, he told me he had seen no cars and the cottages were all empty. And this too, Lieutenant. Derechy was on welfare and suddenly he became a free spender, treating people at The Red Wheel taproom."

"Sounds reasonable," Newpole said. "Especially when Derechy has taken his car and made tracks fast."

"When?"

"This morning. Even before the shooting started. His wife says he left as soon as you and Rigsby drove by their cottage and entered the woods. That's when he beat it."

"Is there a G.A. out on him?"

"Oh, yes," Newpole said, putting his cold pipe into his pocket. "They'll pick up Derechy somewhere. But there are still a few holes in the case. For one thing, we have no line on the robbery money. Maybe we'll find it on Derechy when he's taken. If we don't, he's the type who'll sing like a little dickey bird." He glanced at me. "You look a little tired and dirty, Ralph. All pooped out?"

"A little," I admitted. "I was supposed to go on my day off this afternoon. I think I'd better see the sergeant."

I didn't go on a day off. Neal told me that all my days off were cancelled until further notice. He did give me a break, though. As long as I had no patrols until the next morning he would let me have an eight-hour night pass. But I had to write my report first.

I did that. By the time was I through it was 10.00 p.m. I turned the report in, showered, shaved and dressed in civilian clothes. When I went down into the parking lot for my car, I headed towards the one place I wasn't supposed to go. The Red Wheel.

It wasn't that I was deliberately trying to get into trouble again. I had enough trouble as it was. But Lieutenant Newpole had said there were a few holes in the case.

I knew what one of them was. I had the silver cobweb in my pocket.

CHAPTER NINETEEN

IT WAS SATURDAY night and The Red Wheel was crowded. Quite a few newspapermen were in the taproom and one of them recognised me. I told him I wasn't news and that I didn't know any more than he did. He hung on a little, unbelievingly, then let me go.

When Amy Bell came on, I moved out of the taproom and stood in the foyer watching her. She played the piano and sang several numbers, but her voice was listless and had lost its vibrant tremor. She seemed mechanical in her actions. The other patrons sensed the change in her, too, because the dining-room was quite noisy when she sang. When she went off with a quick bow, the applause was scattered and half-hearted. I gave a note to a waiter to take to her dressing-room, telling her I wanted to see her in the taproom.

When I went back to the taproom, Harry gave me a busy, cheery hello as he deftly mixed drinks along with two white-coated assistants. I ordered a bourbon and soda just to have something in my hand. There was a little argument with Harry when I insisted on paying for it. But I did pay.

I leaned half on the stool and half on the counter, sipping on the drink, not thinking of anything or anybody except Amy Bell. Somebody patted my back. I turned around and saw Carl Podre standing behind me.

He said, " What's this I hear about you paying for your drink? "

" The boss wants it that way," I said. " In my business you don't argue with the captain."

" You work for a bunch of stiff-necks," Podre said. " What the hell do they think I'm going to do? Corrupt you? "

" They're cops," I said. " Cops have suspicious minds."

He laughed. " Hell, after doing the Hozak job to-day, they ought to give you the State House. Kid, you're hotter than a two-dollar pistol. You're really going high, wide and handsome. I mean it. Look around. The town's jumping with joy and the place is loaded with newsmen. What do you say? I'll let them know you're here and we'll take some pictures."

" That's out," I said. " I didn't do the job, Carl. It was Kerrigan."

" What the hell, you were with him, weren't you? "

" Not me. All I did was get in a jam."

" How? "

" Some day I'll tell you all about sticky pine-tree sap. I'm going to make a study of it."

He looked puzzled for a moment, then laughed. I suppose he thought I had meant to say something funny and he laughed to be polite about it.

" How's Amy? " I asked.

" Not so good, Ralphie."

" What's the matter? "

" I don't know. She's 'way off form to-night. Did you hear her? "

" Yes," I said. " What do you think is wrong with her? "

" Beats the hell out of me," he said. " She's been that way since the other day when she went riding with you."

" She tell you about that? "

" She tells me nothing. I called her at Danziger's and the old lady told me. Did you two have a fight? "

" No," I said. " There was no fight."

" I don't know what's got into her. She stays in her dressing-room. She won't come out and mix. These girls, they begin to get a little name and they start getting temperamental on you. Always happens. The best of them become bitchy."

I turned on the stool. " I wouldn't want anybody to call Amy bitchy," I said. " Not anybody. Not even you, Carl."

He smiled quickly. " Don't bulge your muscles at me, Ralphie. Relax. I was talking about entertainers in general, not Amy. What's the matter with you? "

"Nothing. I don't always like the way you talk, Carl."

"Look, Ralphie, take it from an old friend. You're wasting your time with Amy. I mean it from the heart. You're reaching for something you can't have. It's out of your class."

"What do you mean by class, Carl?"

"You know what I mean. This girl moves in different circles now. She meets the big money, the fast spenders, the Las Vegas-Palm Springs-Miami crowd. Sure, you're a good-looking kid and you look real sharp in your tailored uniform. But what can you *give* her?"

"Give? Dammit, why does it have to be *give* all the time? What if two people love each other?"

"Ralphie boy," he said pityingly. "What's with this cornball love business? You go down to the slums and you see these faded, worn-out women with their hordes of brats. You ever see love between them and their husbands? Their husbands are down at the corner saloon lapping up beer because they can't afford whisky. They stay there all night. They don't want to go home to a crappy house filled with squalling kids who are eating up every nickel of their paycheck. Ralphie, money brings love. You ask any of the big-money boys. They'll tell you there's nothing like a mink coat to make a woman real sexy. I mean it. Any psychologist will tell you that money, diamonds and furs do something chemical to a woman."

"Not the way I studied chemistry."

"This is a different kind of chemistry, Ralphie. It's a new world. New values. To-day you buy love like you buy a pair of shoes."

"Then I don't like the new world," I said.

"So play it your own way. But, if I were you, I wouldn't include Amy in my plans."

"Don't figure everybody by your own values, Carl."

"I'm not. Look, you sent Amy a note to her dressing-room, didn't you?"

"You've got a good spy system, Carl."

"Sure, my waiters. They work for *me*, not you, Ralphie. They tell me everything that goes on. So you sent Amy a note to meet you here in the tap-room. Has she shown?"

"She'll show."

"She's cooled off on you," he said. "A girl might get a little excited at first. Then she starts to think of the size of your monthly paycheck."

"Don't sneer at my paycheck," I said. "I'm no fifty-dollar-a-week cop. I can support a wife."

"I know. They pay you pretty good and it gets better as you go along. But these girls go for the *big* money, Ralphie. The big dough. When you're in the twenty-five-thousand-a-year class then you talk to them."

"You mean you're in a position to talk to Amy?"

"Nothing personal, Ralphie." He waved his hand, encompassing The Red Wheel. "This place makes money."

"If it was all yours. You don't own this club, Carl."

"I've got a piece of it. Some day it'll be mine." He patted my back. "You're all right, kid. Just shorten your sights a little. There's a dame for every man in this world."

" I'll wait right here for Amy," I said.

" She won't show, Ralphie," he said, starting to walk away. " I'll lay you odds, ten to one."

" She'll show," I said stubbornly.

But he was right. She didn't show. I waited at the bar for over an hour, sipping on that one glass of bourbon, watching Harry as he worked.

Then Amy went on stage again and I moved out into the foyer to watch her. She sang only two hurried songs and by then it was midnight. The bar closed. The last few stragglers were finishing their drinks and Harry and his assistants were tidying up.

I left the taproom. The dining-room was empty and Carl Podre was gone. I asked a waiter where I could find the dressing-room. He showed me. I went around by the kitchen and into a narrow corridor. There was a flimsy, laminated wooden door with a little gold star pasted on it. I knocked.

" Who is it? " Amy's voice asked.

" Ralph," I said.

" Go away," she said.

" Open the door or I'll lean on it and push it down."

I waited. There was the sound of a lock being unfastened and the door opened. She was wearing a white towel around her head turban-style, a blue silk robe and blue slippers. Her face was white and smooth, with traces of cold cream near her hairline.

" So you're a real tough one," she said. " As much as you've tried to hide it, that cop mentality sticks out all over you. Or do they give you a special course in breaking down doors to ladies' boudoirs? "

" Maybe you're more familiar with the wolf system," I said. " What do your wolf friends do? Huff and puff like in the nursery rhyme? "

" If that's meant as a nasty crack," she said, " you can get out of here."

But I moved past her and stepped inside. There was a dressing-table. Above it, surrounded by lighted bulbs, was a mirror. She went over to it and sat down. With a sheet of tissue she began wiping cold cream from her face.

" I sent you a note," I said.

" I haven't paid attention to notes since I was in the fourth grade."

" I sent you a note," I said. " You didn't have to stay in here and sulk."

" Sulk? What do I have to sulk about? I'm lovely, I'm becoming famous, I use cold cream."

" You could have sent me an answer," I said. " A brush-off like this isn't cricket. It's not according to the rules of the game."

" I don't owe you a thing, dear," she said. " I didn't brush you off, because there was nothing to brush off. Not even a tiny piece of lint."

" Not lint. You mean some of that sticky, gooey stuff you called love."

" There's nothing," she said. " There never was anything. You walked me home one night and you took me for a ride one afternoon. That doesn't buy you one teeny-weeny part of me. So don't flatter yourself, dear."

" You're lying," I said amiably. " I have a feeling towards you. I wouldn't have it unless you felt the same way about me."

"Like an electric charge," she said, laughing shortly. "You feel vibrations."

"I don't know what it is. But it's there and you know it's there."

"Don't get tangled up in my life," she said. "I don't sleep well when I get emotional. It affects my voice."

"The hell with your voice," I said amiably.

"The hell with you," she said. "I have to get dressed."

"Go right ahead," I said.

"Look, Junior," she said. "This isn't the Shubert Theatre where the man stands there in his top hat and white tie and the star gets behind a screen and says very gay things while she tosses her stockings and garter belt over the top. This is the sticks. And, as you can see, there's no screen."

"I don't mind about the screen," I said. "I like it better without the screen."

"Outside," she said.

I went outside. She locked the door.

CHAPTER TWENTY

I WAITED OUTSIDE in the corridor, leaning against the wall. In ten minutes she came out. She was dressed in a prim, dove-grey suit and black shoes.

"You look like a business woman," I said, "not like a glamorous singing star."

"I'm more of a business woman than you think," she said. "Good night dear. I have a date."

"You have a date with me," I said.

"I have a date with a four-poster bed. It's one o'clock in the morning. I've refused six different dates to-night. You're a seven-time loser, dear."

"Seven is my lucky number," I said. "My car is in the parking lot."

"Good-bye, dear. I'm not going with you. Have fun and all that."

I smiled at her. "Sure, you're going with me. You're scared and you're panicky and you're running away from something. I know what's behind it, honey. That's why we'll take a ride and you'll tell me all about it."

"Well, well," she said. "A new twist. An amateur mind reader. If you know some dark deep secret about me, suppose you tell me right now. That will clear it up, won't it?"

"No," I said. "That wouldn't solve it. You have to volunteer it yourself. Otherwise we'll still have the problem."

"All right," she said. "I know when I'm licked. I'm a notorious dope queen from Ypsilanti. The police of fourteen states are hot on my trail. Are you satisfied now?"

"Let's take the ride, honey. You'll tell me."

"What if I don't?"

"Then we'll have to do it the hard way."

"What way?"

"We'd have to go to the barracks, Amy. I wouldn't like it and you wouldn't like it."

"Now you're pulling rank on me," she said.

"I have no choice."

"You're bluffing, of course. But I'll go along. It'll

be just for curiosity, dear. I'm mad about puzzles."

We went out to the parking lot. She looked at my battered old Ford. "Isn't it jazzy?" she said. "I haven't been in a jalopy since I was seventeen."

"Let's not be undemocratic," I said, helping her in.

"Oh, no, I'm honoured. The evening papers were full of a furious gun battle between the notorious 'Slicker' Hozak, the famed Trooper Ralph Lindsey, and some inconsequential corporal named Philip Kerrigan. You've made the town of Dorset safe to live in again. Hi, killer. Or have you grown sensitive about those things?"

I started the car. "Not me." I grinned. "I didn't fire a shot. It was Kerrigan. I was sort of a dumb sitting duck, a decoy."

"Then the newspapers were very kind to you. They gave you fifty per cent of the credit. Didn't Kerrigan mind?"

"Tickled silly. The real truth would have been very embarrassing to the State Police."

"Now I suppose you're taking me to your favourite necking spot along the pond."

"No," I said. I didn't tell her it was too near the Derechy house, where there was a stake-out in case Derechy came back. "We'll go to Parker River in Rowley. But I'm forgetting my duties as a host. You must be hungry."

"Only for your arms, dear."

I grinned in the dark.

"I saw that very engaging smile," she said. "Let me tell you right now that charm won't work. I can't stay long. I've got to get some sleep because I'm leaving town the first thing to-morrow."

"Oh," I said. "I thought your engagement here ran another week."

"Cancelled out," she said. "I'm going to New York."

"Sudden, isn't it?"

"When the mood strikes the artist, you know——"

"Doesn't Carl mind?"

"Not at all. I've been off my feed a little.'

"But why New York? I thought your next engagement was at Salisbury Beach."

"I cancelled it. I have a tryout in a musical. Aren't I the lucky one?"

"No," I said. "There's no tryout in New York. You're running away."

She didn't answer that.

I drove out across U.S. 1 on to the Rowley Road, winding around, crossing the dark, sleeping town and over a little stone bridge. I turned to the right. The moon gleamed on the river. I pulled up under some trees and stopped.

She said, "You know all the intimate places where loving couples can entwine."

"Extensive research," I said. "I'm beginning to pay attention to small details."

"What do we do now?" she asked. "Turn the radio on to soft music and wait for a cloud to hide the moon before we start wrestling?"

"No," I said, "first you take this."

I took the silver brooch from my pocket and put it in her lap. She stared down at it, not moving.

"Take it, it's yours," I said. "And don't tell me it isn't. Every time you lie your ears turn pink."

" You can't see my ears in the dark."

" I'll bring out my flashlight," I said.

She picked up the brooch and ran her fingers over the thin cobweb strands. " It's such a worthless bauble to make a fuss about."

" But it's yours," I said. " That's the point I want to make."

" All right, it's mine," she said with sudden vehemence. " So what does it prove? That I was at the pond last summer, parking with somebody? "

" More than that," I said. " Next I want you to tell me why you found it necessary to lie about it."

" Because I thought you were the insanely jealous type. If you knew I had been to that sacred spot with another Romeo you might have throttled me."

I smiled at her. " This isn't a tryout for a musical comedy, honey. This happens to be for keeps."

" No laughs? "

" No laughs," I said. " A twenty-one-year-old girl has been murdered. The kind of girl you see every day in every town. A pretty girl who wouldn't harm a flea. Next, a twenty-two-year-old boy was murdered. He was important, too. Even though he didn't care much about living after the girl was killed. That's why there are no laughs in this honey."

" I'm sorry," she said, her voice muted. " Will you believe I'm really and truly sorry? "

" Yes," I said. " I believe you. We're getting along fine now, Amy. We've established the fact that you were at Dorset Pond last summer. The next question is who was the man with you? "

" My lips are forever sealed. He is now married and has five lovely children. The oldest boy is——"

She broke off and buried her face in her hands. "There I go again," she said, her voice muffled. "I don't know what's the matter with me. I can't help it."

"I know," I said. "Everytime you get into a tight corner you try to laugh it off."

"It's to stop the tears from coming to my eyes. I'm the original Pagliacci."

"Maybe I should remind you of this, Amy. I know who the man is, but I have to hear it from you."

"I'm getting terribly weary of this game."

"It's not a game. You know it isn't a game. Give me his name."

Her hands twisted around the brooch. "His name is Carl Podre. There. Does it give you a sadistic pleasure to have made me say it?"

"No. It gives me no pleasure at all. What's the rest of it?"

"Nothing. I was lonesome and he took me riding. We held hands and ate popcorn like two depraved characters."

"Strike the last sentence," I said. "I want the rest of it."

"There is no more."

"Yes, there is. There's the part where the fear comes in, the scared-rabbit look, the running away. A date with Carl Podre a year ago didn't cause all that."

"It's you, dear. I just tremble when your masculinity comes near me."

"We can sit here and swap wisecracks until dawn. But we'll just be wasting time. I'll say it once more. You'll have to tell me. Otherwise, I'm afraid you're going to be in a bit of a mess."

" That's all there is, dear. I've told you everything."

" I can wait for the answer," I said. " I'm in no particular hurry."

" Fine," she said. " I propose to fight it out on this line if it takes all summer. Didn't a famous general say that? "

" U. S. Grant. But he had a bigger army than you, honey. You're fighting this alone."

She cuddled in against me, her head resting in the hollow of my shoulder. I put my arm around her, bent and brushed my lips against her scented hair.

" I'm so weary," she said. " I could fall asleep in your arms."

" Go ahead," I said. " When you wake up you'll feel better. Then you'll tell me."

" It means that much to you? "

" Yes. Everything has to be clean and honest between us. I might want to marry you some day."

Her head turned up to me. " I thought you said no more wisecracks? "

" It's not a wisecrack, Amy."

" I said before you were a young man in a hurry. You seem to have made up your mind very quickly."

" When the opportunity strikes, you have to grab it. I might never meet another one like you."

" It's spring. Love is in the air."

" For you, too? "

" Not quite, dear. I'm older and I've fought it every inch of the way. I'll admit you have a habit of sending little shivers up my spine. But it's no good for me and I know it'll never work out. That's another reason I'm leaving. I don't want any foreign entanglements."

" You're fighting a natural feeling, honey."

" I know. Why do you think I wanted you to stay away from me? I don't want to be carried away by emotion. I'm not ready for marriage. Nor for the little vine-covered cottage and the mortgage that goes with it."

" Maybe it's a different type of marriage you want. The money marriage. The Cadillac convertible, the three mink coats in the closet, the houseman in white coat and silver buttons. The paunchy, bald-headed husband who's been twice divorced or widowed, so every time you go to bed you have to take a stiff slug of brandy so you won't be sick about it. Is that what you really want? If it is, tell me straight."

" You think I'm like that? " she asked.

" No, I don't. Not you. There are a lot of people who think that way. But not you. If I thought you were like them I wouldn't be here now."

" Thank you, dear. No, it's not that. It's the itch inside me. The career. Amy Bell in lights. Amy Bell in a hit Broadway musical. Amy Bell in pictures, in CinemaScope. Amy Bell on television singing to forty million people. That's the itch. It gnaws right into my heart."

" Nobody ever gave you a guarantee any of that would happen. It could end up the other way. In a strip joint in the Chicago Loop, singing for pennies, mixing with a lot of dirty, unwashed, foul-mouthed drunks, so they'll buy more drinks. And every once in a while a customer in an upstairs room for another few bucks. It could end that way, too."

" I know. But I have to have my chance. It's there. I've made my start. You have no right to cut me off from it."

" We'd make a nice couple," I said.

" A lovely couple."

" Sleeping in a barracks wouldn't be half-bad if I knew, when I came home, you'd be waiting at the little swinging gate for me."

" And how often would you come home? "

" About every four days."

" And what if I didn't want you away from me four days at a time? What if I wanted you home every night? Would *you* make the sacrifice? "

" Yes. I don't have to be a trooper. It takes five minutes to resign."

" You'd do all that for me? "

" Well, I'm not a very good cop, anyway. I think they'd be happy to take up a collection and give me a big send-off."

" I don't know what you're talking about. You're a very good trooper. You stick to the State Police and let me stick to my career." She looked up at me. " Can't you see, dear? It wouldn't work. The vine-covered cottage would pall on me. I'd sit there and eat my heart out because you took me away from the bright lights, from the brilliant career. It might start out all lovey-dovey, but soon I'd be blaming you because you took me away from my big chance. I'd picture myself on Broadway or in Hollywood, all slick and glamorous instead of being a grubby house-wife. I'd blame you for everything that went wrong. I'd begin to hate you."

" I'd remind you of the strip joint in the Chicago Loop."

" I wouldn't believe it," she said. " I'd dream the other dream. I'm sorry, dear, but I've got to keep going. I have to make my try." She squeezed my hand. "Now if you'll take your prisoner home, dear——"

I looked out into the darkness for a moment. "There's still some unfinished business," I said. "We stay here until it's cleared. We ended with you and Carl Podre on the bluff near the pond. That was last summer. We've got to bring it up to date."

She sighed. "I'm very tired, dear. Can't we postpone it until to-morrow?"

"To-morrow will be too late, Amy."

She squeezed her eyes, then opened them. "Do you mind if I catch an hour's sleep in your arms?"

"No," I said. "Maybe it would do a lot of good. You'd wake up with a refreshed mind and a better recollection."

She curled up, her legs under her, resting her head on my shoulder. I sat there looking out into the night, at the silently moving, luminous band of the river. Soon she was breathing slower and more deeply.

The minutes ticked by, then an hour. She slept on. I thought of many things. Of Amy Bell, in my arms, wanting a career above everything, who wanted to run away in her determination to save it. Of Carl Podre and his bland smoothness and false affability. Of Trooper Keith Ludwell, who was also concerned with a career and who was relentless, ruthless and calculating every inch of the way. Of an eager, intense waitress named Marsha Gordioni, who would hope in vain but would never marry Keith Ludwell. Of two murdered youngsters named Mary Ann Fedder and Russell Westlake, who had done nothing more than to appear at a certain spot at a certain time. Of granite-faced Captain Roger Dondera, who did not tolerate mistakes in judgment.

Then there was a foul ball named Ralph Lindsey, who had made mistakes in judgment and who was accident-prone. He was being investigated and his transfer to another barracks would probably go through in twenty-four hours. I thought of my paraplegic father, " Old Walt " Lindsey, imprisoned in a wheel-chair, dying by degrees, whose only joy left in life was to sit and talk to me about my work and what he would have done in the same circumstances. Always watching my progress and giving me advice. And when my quick transfer came through, the light would die in his eyes and the hope would go out of him. He would not say anything about it because he would understand that my career would not rise and there would be no need for further explanation. For him it would be over.

And I thought of Amy Bell again. And three bank robbers. The first man, the fast-talking, conscience-less, glib killer named Kurt Swenke. The second man, the dead, brainy George " Slicker " Hozak, whose cleverness ended with a bullet from a Win-chester rifle. And the third man, sloppy, cowardly, cunning-eyed Joe Derechy, who was on the run.

And I thought of the fourth man who was on the loose, too.

CHAPTER TWENTY-ONE

THE HOURS SLIPPED BY and the sky in the east grew lighter. A mist formed along the river and spread to the low-lying fields, covering them like a woolly grey-white blanket. Once Amy stirred, clutched me fiercely and muttered something indistinct. The sky grew brighter and the mist dissipated in wisps. The clouds in the sky turned pink, the river and trees taking form. Then the sun came up over the horizon, a big red ball, and Amy moved, opened her eyes and sat up with a start.

" Good lord," she said. " We still here? "

" Yes."

" I slept hours. Did I say anything in my sleep? "

" No."

" Let me have a cigarette, please. And what time is it? "

" After six."

I handed her a cigarette and lit it for her. She drew on it deeply, twice, then cast it out. Her hands went to her face and hair, touching here and smoothing there. Then she opened her compact, looked into a tiny mirror and put on lipstick. I watched her.

She brushed at her clothes, stretched and said, " Are you going to take me home now? "

" No. Time is up, Amy, but I can't take you home. You'll have to go to the barracks with me."

" And what other alternative do I have? "

" You could tell me what I want to know."

" Even if it ruins everything for me? "

" No. It would be the best way, honey."

" There's nothing I could offer you? "

" What could you offer me, Amy? "

She let her breath out, her face flushing. " No, I couldn't offer you anything, could I? I realise that now. All I'm doing now is becoming more disgusted with myself."

" Tell me all about it," I said. " Time is growing very short."

" Yes," she said. " Could I have another cigarette, please? "

I gave her another cigarette, lighting it for her, watching as she dragged deeply on it.

She said, " Don't look at me while I talk. I'd rather you didn't look at me, And I wish I had a stiff double brandy."

I lit a cigarette, my head turned away. " I'm not looking at you, honey. Talk."

" You know Carl gave me my first chance," she said. " I was grateful—oh, so grateful. It meant everything to me and Carl knew it. He made sure I was grateful and showed appreciation. Never let it be said that Carl Podre never capitalised on a situation. Well, you know the sordid words and music. It's as old as life itself."

" Go on," I said.

" Carl lives in a bungalow behind The Red Wheel. He wanted me to move in there. I said I wouldn't. If I had to sleep with him I didn't want the towns-people or the club employees to know. I didn't have to degrade myself that much. So he suggested a motel somewhere. But I said no again. The motel owners would know him. Some day if I ever made the big-time they'd remember me, too."

She looked at the glowing cigarette tip. "But Carl was in there pitching. If I insisted on discretion he knew of an abandoned cabin on Dorset Pond. The owner had moved to Tennessee and the cabin wasn't in use. We went there. The windows were covered with boiler plating, but Carl loosened one of them and got inside. We stayed there that night. And another night, and another night. The fourth night there we had a fight. It was something rather personal and I'd rather not tell you. I ran out of the cottage towards the road and he chased me and grabbed me and we wrestled a little and he tore my dress and that's how I lost the silver brooch. But I didn't go back to the cottage. I told him I wouldn't. He let it rest. I never went there again. I finished my engagement and left on other bookings."

"But you came back this year."

"Yes. Back to the lion's den again. He wrote me and offered me a great deal more money. He said the customers were asking for me. I had a few weeks before going to Salisbury Beach. My agent wired him back and told him I would come. But I also phoned Carl. I told him it was strictly singing and nothing else. I was very emphatic about it. He agreed and I came. I swear he never touched me this time."

"But he tried."

"He tried, but he never touched me. Not this time. I swear."

"You didn't have to come back. Not for a lousy few weeks' engagement."

"I know," she said. "But I chalked last summer

up to experience and education. Besides, I was flattered that he needed me and the customers had asked for me. And, frankly, I could use the money."

" Those were the *only* reasons? "

" No. There was still another reason. I had left Carl on a sour note last summer. He has a gutter code of ethics. I was afraid he might write my other bookings a chatty note and tell them I was a good roll in the hay."

" What if he did? That wouldn't mean they'd believe him."

" You don't understand, dear. I'm a female entertainer—a solo, not part of a team. I'm fair game. You have to expect to be fair game. I can fight it if I'm not handicapped. But if Carl sent out the word, I'd have no weapon. The word would go along from booking to booking. I didn't want to take that chance. This way everything would end on a friendly, platonic basis. He hired my voice and nothing else. Carl was satisfied and so was I."

" So he pressured you into coming back," I said.

" He hinted it very strongly. Not in so many words, of course. But I could gather the inference."

" Yes," I said slowly. " I guess Carl would do a thing like that without batting an eye. But somebody else knew about you and Carl going to that cabin. Another person."

" Yes. Joe Derechy. He lives near there. He's the big ugly brute who made the remarks the other night in the taproom."

" I know. Was he pretty friendly with Carl? "

" He used to do some handyman work for Carl. I don't think they were social friends." She turned to me. " How did you know about all this? "

"Well, it's something you pick up bit by bit. Then when you put all the pieces together, suddenly you have something. For example, too much fuss made over a little silver brooch. A chance remark some cop made about a gangster's mother who said her son was friendly with a priest. It could be possible that she mistook some handwriting on a postcard, translating the word *Podre* into *padre*. But it doesn't matter. You were pretty jumpy when we rode out to the pond that day. You kept looking at the abandoned cottage and I kept remembering Carl Podre telling me he had been very friendly with you last summer."

"Yes. The cottage had no fond memories for me. I wanted to wash it from my mind. When you found the brooch, I denied it was mine. I'd have denied anything about that place. But somebody must have seen you and me there because they told Carl."

"Joe Derechy," I said.

"Of course. Now that I stop to think of it, who else? He could see us from his cottage."

"Yes. So he told Carl and Carl came to you. What did Carl say?"

"He said it would be best if I never mentioned the cottage to you, or anything about it. He said he had known you since you were a child and you might snicker about it and it wouldn't do any of us a bit of good. Of course I agreed heartily. I didn't want anybody to know about my dirty linen. Then he asked me again yesterday if I had said anything. I said no. I hadn't even seen you. He said he was wondering because you had been poking around with Chief Rigsby."

"Didn't that make you suspicious?" I asked.

" You must have known there was something odd about the cottage if Carl was so concerned about it."

" Yes, I had an idea something was wrong. But I didn't know what it was."

" But you finally found out, didn't you? "

" Yesterday, for the first time. When you and that corporal killed Hozak. The radio said he had been hiding out at the cottage. Then I knew Derechy and also Carl must have had something to do with it. And when they linked Hozak to the murderer, Swenke, I began to get terribly frightened."

" Because it also tied Carl Podre in with the murders."

" No, not because of that. The thing began to get too big for me. I knew I had to get out, and fast. Last night I told Carl I was leaving. He was relieved to hear it."

" Why was he so relieved? "

" He said the police might find out about us using the cottage and it wouldn't do my reputation or his any good. He also swore he knew nothing about the murders, or Swenke, or Hozak. He hadn't been to the cottage since last year, and it was only a coincidence that Hozak had used it. After all, he said, a lot of other people knew about the abandoned cottage."

" And you believed him? "

" I wanted to believe him. I had to believe him."

" As a sop to your own conscience? "

" No, dear."

" Yes. Because you were going to walk out and let Carl Podre and Joe Derechy continue on the loose. They *could* have had something to do with the murders. Didn't *that* bother you? "

"That wasn't my job. I'm not a cop. You are."

"It *was* your job, Amy. You know that. You've known that since you were a child and learned right from wrong. And how do you think cops work? Sitting in a chair with fingertips pressed together, contemplating? Or guessing about things? They work on information, Amy."

She didn't answer. I flipped my cigarette away and said, "Okay, what else did Carl confide in you? Did he tell you about being a silent partner in a bank robbery in Newburyport so he could buy The Red Wheel? Or that he used his station wagon to lug a stove down to the water so he could tie Westlake's body to it?"

Her eyes widened. "My lord, no."

"Maybe he told you about some anonymous letters. How he wrote them to wreck a man's career. Letters about me because I knew what he was. Because I was just tanglefooted enough to stumble on to something and he wanted to get rid of me. Or maybe you yourself wrote the letters for him."

"No, Ralph," she said. "You mean you actually think those terrible things about me?"

"Dammit, I don't want to. But you could have come to us with what you knew."

"I didn't know anything," she cried. "What happened between me and Carl happened a year ago. There were no murders then, no bank robbery. Just a sordid little interlude." Her head drooped. "All right, I had suspicions. But that's all they were— suspicions. Nothing else."

"Enough to come to us with."

"No. I had only tiny fragments of it. How can you

tell what was going on in my mind? " Then suddenly tears welled in her eyes and dribbled down her cheeks. I took out my handkerchief and gave it to her.

She dabbed at her cheeks and eyes. " I'm sorry," she said. " I couldn't let it touch me. No matter how innocent, how remote my contact was with this thing, the newspapers would play it up. *Night Club Singer Tells All. Gangster's Moll Talks to Cops. Singer Reveals Love Tryst With Killer.* How would all that sound to a booking agent? I couldn't get a job singing in a hamburger stand in Scollay Square. I had the right to protect my career. I had, I had. You can't hold that against me."

" I'm not holding it against you," I said. " Not now. The important thing is that you told me yourself. Once you did that you shifted sides. I had to make sure where you stood."

" And what happens now? " she asked, her voice shaky.

" You're not with them. You never were. So everything is fine."

" You'll cover for me? "

" Don't worry about it."

" I trust you, dear. I trust you more than anybody I ever met."

" Don't worry," I said. " Put a smile on your face. I'm driving you home."

CHAPTER TWENTY-TWO

I LET HER OFF at Mrs. Danziger's. She stood there uncertainly as though she didn't want to go in, as though it was all a trick and she didn't believe she was actually free. Then she dragged herself listlessly up the stairs to the front door.

I waved cheerily to her and drove off. As soon as I got around the corner, I stopped again. Taking the S. & W. from the holster I checked the cylinder. When I was finished I didn't put the revolver back in its holster. I slipped it into my jacket pocket. Then I started the car and drove over to The Red Wheel.

I went by the deserted parking lot to a narrow side street that ran parallel to the club. Half-way down I parked the Ford. Stepping out I looked around. I was at the back of The Red Wheel, facing an alley which was empty except for three battered garbage cans.

The street was quiet and empty and there was a smell of fresh dew on the grass. Behind the alley was a small grey bungalow, a gravel path leading to it.

I walked up the path to the front door. Fastened to it was a brass plate with the name *Carl Podre*. I rang the bell, hearing its sharp twang through the house. I waited. No answer.

Moving away, I went around the back. I tried the bell there, hearing a buzz. Nobody answered it. I tried the door. Locked. I went to the front, passing windows with drawn venetian blinds. There was no station wagon around and that made me a little anxious. I rang the front bell again. I knocked at the door, then hammered on it. I tried the knob. It was locked. I waited, listening for the slightest sound inside. Dead silence.

I came out of the side street to the entrance of The Red Wheel. There was no bell. The door was locked. I looked into the window nearest the door. All I could see was an empty dining-room, with up-ended chairs on bare tables. I turned around and looked down Main Street. For the first time, I noticed a dusty black sedan parked under some trees thirty yards away.

I walked over to it. Detective-Lieutenant Gahagan was sitting behind the wheel smoking a pipe.

" Hello, Ralph," he said calmly. " Kind of early to be going in for a short beer, isn't it? "

" Dammit," I said.

" What's the matter, Ralph? "

" You're staked out for Podre, aren't you? "

" Sure," Gahagan said.

" Where is he, Lieutenant? "

" You won't find him around here. Your friend has flown the coop. The place is closed down pending a search warrant. What were *you* going to do? "

" Hell," I said. " I was going to be a hero, Lieutenant. Pictured myself bring Podre in by the scruff of the neck and saying, ' Here I cleaned it up for you.' "

" You're about an hour too late," Gahagan said imperturbably. " The Connecticut State Police picked up Derechy on the Post Road during the night. He's been singing his song at G.H.Q. "

" What did he say, Lieutenant? "

" He admitted he and Podre dumped Westlake's body

into the pond. They used Podre's station wagon. The pickup order on Podre came in about an hour ago. We missed him by five minutes, but we know where he is.'

" Where, Lieutenant? "

" They cut him off on 133 near the West Boxford line. He scooted out of his station wagon and into the woods. How did you know about Podre? "

" Sir," I said, " I have my own informant."

" You'd better get the hell back to the barracks," Gahagan said. " Every man's been called back from time off. They've gone in to flush him out."

" I'm on my way," I said.

The only trooper in the barracks was Corporal Phil Kerrigan. He was at the short-wave radio talking to the dispatcher at Framingham. He looked over his shoulder, shook his head at me and told me I was late.

" We called your home," he said. " You're supposed to leave an address when you're given a pass."

" Sorry," I said. " I only expected to be gone a couple of hours. It took longer than I planned."

" Podre——" he started to say.

" I know," I said. I had been pulling off my tie. Now I was unbottoning my jacket and shirt. " I met Lieutenant Gahagan at The Red Wheel."

" All right, change over and get out there. You'll find the captain out on 133 at the West Boxford line. Take a bike. Number Fourteen. There isn't a cruiser left in the joint. Okay, kid, hit it."

I clattered upstairs into my room, changed swiftly and ran down again buckling my gunbelt. Down the stairs to the garage. I warmed up the motor-cycle and sped out of there in a roar.

It was a little cool for motor-cycle riding but I drove fast, the wind whipping at my face. I cut off Route 1 on to 97, going through the little town of East Boxford until I reached Georgetown. From there I turned off on to 133, passing along the edge of the forest.

Seeing a light blue tunic ahead of me, I slowed down. It was Tony Pellegrini by the side of the road, standing straddle-legged, a Winchester rifle in his hands. He waved and motioned me on. I passed him and came to Trooper Driscoll a hundred yards ahead. He was facing the woods and holding a riot gun. Then I came upon a cluster of cars. There were some plain-clothes men and the Georgetown police, Captain Dondera and his second-in-command, Lieutenant McQuade.

I pulled over and stopped. I set the bike on its kick stand and went over to Captain Dondera.

"You're late," he said. "Go down the road and you'll see Sergeant Neal. He'll assign you a post."

"Yes, sir," I said. I went back to the bike, started it and drove farther down the road. There I saw a blue cruiser. Sergeant Neal was standing near it, looking into the woods, his head bent toward the open window of the cruiser, listening for radio calls. His holster flap was unbuttoned.

For the third time I heard I was late. Then Neal said, "There's a riot gun for you on the back seat. Take it and go down the road until you see Ludwell. He's just around the bend. Take your post fifty yards beyond him. Get it? Podre is in the woods we're facing. The Andover troopers are over the other side of the woods on 97. The bloodhounds have picked up a scent from the station wagon and they're following Podre's trail. All right, take off."

I grabbed the shotgun and trotted down the road. I came by Wisnioski, then Swanson and Costello. Each was spaced fifty yards apart, each watching the woods. Then I saw Podre's abandoned station wagon with two troopers in plainclothes working over it. One of them was a tech. sergeant from the Framingham Barracks whom I knew. I stopped.

" Did you find anything? " I asked.

The tech. sergeant turned his head. " Soot from a stove," he said. " And a little bit of cash money. Fifty thousand bucks under the front seat. Dondera has that."

" Podre went into the woods here? "

The tech. sergeant pointed. " They tell me he went in over there. The dogs and two Andover troopers went in after him about a half-hour ago."

I trotted down the road again, turning the bend and seeing Ludwell. His face was tense and grim and he was carrying a Thompson submachine gun. I stopped. I heard, for the fourth time, that I was late.

I said, " They told me to take my post fifty yards from you."

He nodded. " Keep going until you're able to see the Boxford police car. Stop there and keep your eyes on the woods. If you spot anything holler out for me."

" Sure," I said. " But I hope I didn't run all the way down here for nothing."

" Why? "

" Well, I've got a personal reason, but I'd like to take Podre myself. The way they're driving him towards Route 97, he won't show back here."

" Don't kid yourself," Ludwell said, his eyes very bright. " Why do you think I picked this spot? Podre knows by now we've got the bloodhounds working."

"How would he know? He can't hear them. The dogs don't make a sound."

"He's smart enough to know we'd call in the dogs," Ludwell said, wetting his lips. "He might not be able to hear them but he'll hear those two troopers who are with the dogs. No matter how careful they are they're bound to make a little noise in the brush."

"That's another reason he won't come out here," I said. "He'll hear the dogs behind him and he'll keep going until he walks right into the men stationed on 97."

"Maybe," Ludwell said. "But maybe he's going to think he can outsmart them. He may try to circle around and double back on his own tracks. Thinks he'll confuse the dogs. The smart ones always try to double back. They're the easiest ones to take."

"How else would you do it?"

"Me, I wouldn't," Ludwell said. "If I knew bloodhounds had my scent and were after me I'd sit down and wait for them because then I'd know the show was over."

I shook my head and left him, turning the final arc in the bend and seeing the snout of the Boxford police car ahead. Beside it was a short, stocky officer in a dark blue uniform. He was watching the woods, too.

I stopped, checked the shotgun, loaded a shell into the chamber and set the safety. Then I faced the woods. I kept looking for something to move. Every once in a while I would see Ludwell as he stepped back on the road for a glance at me.

Time passed. It was very quiet. In the distance I

heard church bells, reminding me it was Sunday morning. The sun rose higher.

Then, suddenly a bird flew up in the woods and screeched angrily. I watched the spot, listening intently. I thought I heard the faint crackle of a twig.

I released the safety of the shotgun and peered into the tangled underbrush. The sound had come from near Ludwell's sector but now there was silence again. I relaxed.

Then, close to the same spot, I heard a swish as though a tree branch had been released and had scraped another. I turned and moved along the road towards it. Silence again. I stopped and waited. Then, a footstep on dry leaves.

I came off the road. There was a slight decline of ground from the shoulder of the highway and I stopped at the bottom of it. The underbrush there was up to my waist. Nothing moved. But I saw a pale yellow-tan patch mingled with the green. I brought up the shotgun and sighted at it.

" Come on out, Carl," I said softly.

The tan patch came closer. I could see Podre now, his pale face streaked with dirt and sweat. The tan patch was a pigskin leather brief-case which he carried in one hand. In the other hand he held an automatic pistol. He was no more than twenty-five feet from me.

" Ralphie," he whispered hoarsely. He moved up a few feet and stopped behind a thick clump of juniper. Now only his head and shoulders were visible. " Ralphie," he said. " I was looking for you. I kept moving along in line with the road, seeing troopers all along the way, hoping I'd spot you out here. Geez, am I glad to see you."

" I'm glad to see you, Carl."

" It's a terrific break. The best break I ever had in my life. Let me through, Ralphie."

" Carl, drop everything you're carrying. Then walk straight towards me with your hands up."

He stared at me. " You're kidding, Ralphie. Let me cross the road. Let me get over to the other side. That's all I ask."

" Don't try it," I said. " This shotgun will tear you apart."

" A break," Podre whispered raspingly. " For my kid brother's sake. For his grave in Korea. Do this one thing for him, Ralphie. This one thing for Paul."

" Your brother's dead," I said. " Don't disgrace him by playing off on his memory. You can't ride on Paul's death forever." I shook my head and my finger tensed on the trigger. " Once more, Carl. Drop the gun and the bag and raise your hands high."

" They've got it all wrong, Ralphie. I had nothing to do with the murder of those two kids. It was Swenke and Hozak. I swear that on Paul's grave. All I did was cover up for them."

" That doesn't buy you a thing, Carl."

" So I'm an accessory. They don't burn you for it." He came out of the juniper bushes, moving three steps forward. " Look, we're old pals from the same neighbourhood, Ralphie. You don't turn in an old pal."

" There was a bank robbery, too, Carl. Add that to the score."

" That's it, kid," he said, talking swiftly, urgently. " Fifty thousand in this brief-case. Half of it's yours. Twenty-five grand to let me cross the road. It's no skin off your nose. You didn't see me. Twenty-five thousand. It would set you up perfect with Amy Bell."

"If I wanted to buy a wife I'd go live in Africa in a mud hut. Come on out, Carl. You've done all your talking."

He was silent for a moment, his head cocked sideways. "Those bloodhounds have turned and they're coming back this way. I'm going through you, Ralphie, and nothing's going to stop me. This automatic holds eight rounds."

"But you won't use it," I said. "Somebody else has always done your shooting for you. Your brother, Paul, in Korea. Swenke and Hozak. Always somebody else, Carl. Now, you do either one of two things. Fire that gun or drop it. Because I'm going to start shooting."

It was odd the way he did it. He dropped the pistol quickly enough. But he held on to the bag for ten seconds before he let it slip through his fingers. Fifty thousand dollars, and he hated to let go of it. He stood there looking down at the bag, then put up his hands and waded through the brush towards me.

I backed out into the middle of the road. When he came up to the edge of it, I told him to turn around with his back to me. He did. Now the Boxford officer had seen us and came running heavily down the road, his police revolver in his hand. When he came up I handed him the shotgun and brought out my service revolver.

I moved in behind Podre. With my free hand I opened my handcuff case, brought down one of his arms and snapped the bracelet on. Then I brought his other hand behind his back and locked both wrists together.

"Thanks," I said to the Boxford officer, taking back the shotgun.

By then Ludwell had seen us and came pelting up. He was so angry that his lips were foam-flecked.

"Damn you," he said, patting Podre's clothes for more weapons. "I told you to holler out."

"Didn't have time, Keith," I said. It was a lie, of course, because I had wanted to do it alone. One more pinch wasn't going to put a halo over my head. I would be transferred out, anyway. This one had been for Amy Bell.

CHAPTER TWENTY-THREE

WHEN I RODE UP on the motor-cycle, she was in the Danziger yard putting a suitcase into her convertible. I climbed off the bike and set it on its kick stand. She was wearing a black whipcord suit and pinned above her breast, gleaming dully, was the silver cobweb.

She watched me, smiled a little hopelessly and wearily and held her wrists out. "It'll be handcuffs, of course," she said tremulously. "You're taking me in, aren't you?"

I grinned. "They do want to see you, Amy."

"Why did I expect you to act differently?" she said tonelessly. "I should have known better."

"Known what, Amy?"

"You were going to give me a break. Don't worry about it, you said. You're on our side. Remember saying those things?"

"I had to speak to them about it, Amy. I had to. Do you understand? You never know about those things. A problem like that needs an older, wiser head than mine."

"I always knew you were all cop, dear," she said bitterly. "Will the newspaper boys be waiting? If they are, I'll change to a real tight sexy dress and dangle a cigarette from the corner of my mouth. I want to look like an authentic gun moll."

"You're all wrong, honey. There'll be no newspaper men. Nobody is going to know. They're pretty decent people. You'll go to the barracks and talk to the captain and a detective named Newpole and a man from the D.A.'s office. Nobody else will be there. All they'll want is your name and address, in case they ever want to reach you. Maybe a few questions."

"Nothing more?"

"Nothing more. You see, Derechy was picked up in Connecticut during the night and Carl Podre was taken this morning. The case is boxed in tight with no loose ends. What you did last summer has nothing to do with it now. It will never come out."

"You're sure, dear? Are you *really* sure?"

"Yes, they told me so."

"And I aged ten years worrying about it. Silly of me, wasn't it, dear?"

"Yes."

"How long will the interview at the barracks take?"

"Shouldn't be more than ten minutes. You're actually leaving now, Amy?"

"Yes, I have another bag to get inside."

I went into the house with her. There was a rich old Oriental rug in the centre hall. On it was a white leather suitcase.

"Why do you have to go?" I asked her.

"I have no more job here, dear. And I do want to get to New York to-day to see my agent."

"You still have that engagement in Salisbury."

She smiled but her eyes were wet. "It would be too close to you. I'd be looking out beyond the spotlights every night, searching for your homely face. I'd be all shivers. I'd look terrible in an off-the-shoulder gown and goose pimples. Besides, you really don't want me, dear. I'm a little tarnished around the edges for a person like you."

"We're all tarnished in some way or other, Amy."

"No, dear. Let me have my chance. Let me go away. Maybe it's out there for me, maybe it isn't. But I have to find out."

"How long will it take?"

"One year, possibly two or three. If it doesn't go, I'll come back."

"You won't come back," I said. "You'll never come back."

"Would you wait?"

"No, Amy," I said. "Because I know you'll never come back."

Her eyes filled again. She put her arms up to me. "I want to kiss you good-bye, dear."

I bent and kissed her. The tears ran down as she stood on her toes and clutched me hard.

She released me. " Good-bye, dear."

" Good-bye, Amy," I said. " I'll carry your bag out."

We went down the three steps of the portico to the car. I put the suitcase into the trunk. She stood there watching me.

I turned to her and touched the silver cobweb. " I see you're wearing it."

" Sort of a gift from you," she said. " Maybe it will bring me luck."

" I hope so," I said. " Good-bye, Amy."

I went back to my motor-cycle and kicked down on the starter. I was thinking of another kind of silver cobweb, one made of bright lights and tinsel and fame and adulation, and Amy Bell was caught in it for ever. The motor-cycle engine started and I drove off. There was no need for me to look back. I knew that was the end of it.

Keith Ludwell wasn't in the dining-room for lunch. I went upstairs to look for him, to check if we were going on patrol together. I didn't see him around.

I came down and went into the duty office for my assignment. Sergeant Neal was behind the desk. He said, " I wanted to talk to you, Ralph."

So that was it, I thought, Ludwell had gone off on patrol without me because my transfer had come through. *Thank you, Trooper Lindsey, you made a couple of lucky pinches but that alone won't put you on the side of the angels. Let some other barracks have the headache with you until your investigation is completed.*

" You're riding with Tony Pellegrini," Neal was

saying. "He's your senior man now. Ludwell has resigned."

I stood stock-still. I knew my mouth gaped but I couldn't do anything about it. "He's what?" I finally asked.

"Resigned. Rather resign than face a court-martial. The reason for his resignation is just between you, me and the captain. You understand?"

"No, Sergeant, I don't."

"Now that's too bad. I'm disappointed, Ralph. All along I thought you were smart. This was right under your nose and you didn't see it."

"Maybe that's why," I said.

"Who do you think wrote those anonymous letters?"

"No," I said. "Ludwell wouldn't do a thing like that." But I was remembering now that since the second letter they had deliberately kept me away from Ludwell.

"It was Ludwell, all right," Neal said. "Stop and think about it, Ralph. In one letter he wrote you were seen leaving a State Police blue cruiser. How many civilians call a police car a cruiser? They call them prowl cars and squad cars and radio cars and police cars."

"Some civilians might call them cruisers."

"Yes. But the letter said a State Police *blue* cruiser. He was differentiating. Only a trooper would know we distinguished between black cruisers and blue cruisers, because our black cruisers look like ordinary sedans and they carry civilian number plates. Most of them don't even have rear radio antennæ like regular police cars do. So who else would know the difference between a black cruiser and a blue cruiser?"

"Yes, sir," I said. "But I don't see where Ludwell could have got the information about the brawl at The Red Wheel. The first time, yes. He saw me with young Cleves. But he wasn't with me on my night off when I had the fight with Derechy."

"Smarten up, Ralph. He had a girl in the diner across from The Red Wheel, didn't he? Marsha Gordioni?"

"Yes," I said slowly.

"The divisional inspector, Captain Reilly, went there. The girl has a good pair of eyes. She was Ludwell's eyes and she wasn't ashamed of it, either. Told Captain Reilly she was kind of proud she was helping Ludwell get ahead. Well, one thing led to another, and up comes the typewriter at the diner that was used for typing menus. There it was in a nutshell. So, if you're smart, Ralph, you'll pick a different diner from now on. The girl might put arsenic in your coffee."

"Ludwell actually wrote those letters?"

"The girl typed them for him. What's the difference? She was only doing what she was told."

"I feel sorry for her," I said. "Honestly, I really do. She was desperately in love with Ludwell." I shook my head. "It's still beyond me, though. I can't understand why Ludwell would want to do it. I thought we were getting along fine."

"He was a young and ambitious man, Ralph. Before you came here he was top man in the barracks. You were a young boot. Your father had quite a name and you came here with a good reputation. You worried Ludwell. He didn't want you to outshine him or get any good assignments, so he simply put the skids to you. Eliminate the competition by taking out the front man."

" All right, so he did it," I said. " He wrote a couple of anonymous letters. So what? You can't blame a man for being a little ambitious. I don't know, but if I were in command, I'd bawl him out, take away some time off, or, at worst, give him a little suspension, and let it go. You're kind of harsh with him, aren't you? "

" Damn right," Sergeant Neal said. " But not only me. The captain and the adjutant and the major and the commissioner. Can you go higher than that? "

" Somebody ought to speak to them."

" You try it. Try going over my head and you won't see a day off in the next two years."

" But Ludwell was a good cop. One of the best. He taught me a lot."

" Nobody's denying he's a good cop. Dammit, he's one of the best troopers I've ever had here. But that's not enough. If he can do this to you, he can stick it into any other trooper who gets in his way. We're a small outfit and every man has to fit. You can't let a man knife a brother officer. Some day, if he wants a conviction badly and the evidence isn't too strong, he might frame a suspect. You want a cop like that working with you, eating with you, living with you? Wondering if he'll run out on you when you're in a tough spot? Wondering when you've sneaked a bottle of beer in here past the corporal that he'll rat on you? Wondering if every pinch he's made is a clean one, or has he framed some drunken bum for a rap that belongs to somebody else just to make his arrest record look good? Would you want to keep worrying about a man like that? "

" No," I said. " I guess not."

" All right. So you ride with Pellegrini and keep your trap shut. It'll leak out, I suppose, but as far as you know, Ludwell quit for personal reasons. You get it? "

" Yes, sir."

" And here's another thing. I expect you to be around this barracks for a while. So when you go on time off you give us an address where we can reach you. No more of that stuff we had this morning."

" Yes, sir."

" Which reminds me. Your punishment has come through. You've lost all time off for a month. Personally, I think they let you off too easy. There'll be no more fights with drunks in public places. I don't care if they insult your grandmother. Understand? "

" Yes, sir."

" When can your father get out here? "

" Next week, if it's all right with you."

" Thursday. Both Kerrigan and I will be here then. I'll have the cook make something special for him. What does he like? "

" Fried chicken and biscuits."

" Fried chicken and biscuits next Thursday," Neal said, making a note on his pad. " Okay, take off. You don't expect Tony to wait all day for you, do you? "

" No, *sir*," I said.

Pellegrini drove. We were in Cruiser 28 driving

along U.S. 1. Pellegrini looked over at me. "So Ludwell went and quit, huh?"

"So I heard," I said. "Must have got a better job."

"He's smart," Pellegrini said, flashing white teeth in a broad smile. "A guy's out of his mind being a trooper."

"I don't see *your* resignation going in," I said.

"Me? I'm crazier than a bedbug. I like the hours. Some weeks, if I try real hard, I put in almost seventy hours. And who do they think they're kidding about Ludwell?"

I smiled back at him, but said nothing.

He said, "How much time off did you lose?"

"A month."

"They must be getting soft. When you lose time off it doesn't go against your record like a suspension. In my day, a public brawl was good for at least a sixty-day suspension."

I grinned at that. *In his day.* Pellegrini was all of twenty-six.

We rode down the turnpike to the Newbury line. There the shortwave radio rasped and said. "K2 to Cruiser 28. A Signal 16 at Dozier Farm in Newbury. Chicken theft. Go ahead, 28."

Pellegrini picked up the handphone and pressed the button. "Received okay. 28 off."

He hung up and shook his head dolefully. "Investigate some stolen chickens. All week we've been living on red meat. Now we've got to go and look for some crummy chickens and get chicken lime all over our nice shiny boots. Well, you wanted to be a trooper, kid. Nobody sent for you."

" You've got take them big and small," I said. " I heard rumours if you crack this one you'll get an extra day off."

" Ha, ha," he said. " I've got a comic riding with me. Listen, I got only one extra day off since I've been with this troop. That was because my mother was sick in the hospital." His teeth flashed again as he made a right turn off the turnpike. " I'll tell you the truth why I'm sticking with this outfit. You can't beat the chow. Real Italian spaghetti and meatballs at least once a month."

" You'll stick," I said. " When they retire you at fifty you'll still be chasing tail-lights."

" Not me, kid. That's twenty-four years from now. Any guy who stays with the State Police that long hasn't got strength enough to ride patrols. I'll be too old and feeble and worn out. The only way they can keep me is to put gold bars on these shoulders and sit me behind a desk at G.H.Q. That I'd like. You ever see some of the girls who work there? "

" At that age you won't be interested in girls."

" Don't kid yourself. As long as I've got eyes in my head I'll be interested in girls. There's a plump little one up on the fifth floor——" He broke off. " How can you think of girls right now? We've got to find those little lost chickens. That's what I don't like about this job. I just had my boots polished and now I'm going into a hen yard and get chicken lime all over them. Why the hell couldn't Danny Driscoll have been riding down here instead of me? "

" What do you have against Driscoll? " I asked.

" Nothing. Only I swear he's got a sixth sense. He took the Peabody-Danvers patrol where he'll

probably run into nice clean felonies like statutory
rape or embezzlement. Me, I have to get chickens."

I laughed. Pellegrini turned his head to me and
began laughing, too, knowing, of course, that I understood him perfectly.

Pellegrini and I would get along fine.

THE END

*Fontana books make available, in attractive, readable yet
inexpensive editions, the best books, both fiction and non-
fiction, of famous contemporary authors. These include books
up to 800 pages, complete and unabridged.*

*If you would like to be kept informed of new and
forthcoming titles please apply to your local bookseller*

or write to

WILLIAM COLLINS SONS & CO. LTD.
144 CATHEDRAL STREET, GLASGOW, C.4.